D0891424

DAMNED BY LOGIC

Recent Titles by Jeffrey Ashford from Severn House

THE COST OF INNOCENCE
CRIMINAL INNOCENCE
DAMNED BY LOGIC
A DANGEROUS FRIENDSHIP
DEADLY CORRUPTION
EVIDENTIALLY GUILTY
FAIR EXCHANGE IS ROBBERY
AN HONEST BETRAYAL
ILLEGAL GUILT
JIGSAW GUILT
JUSTICE DEFERRED
LOOKING-GLASS JUSTICE
MURDER WILL OUT
A TRUTHFUL INJUSTICE
A WEB OF CIRCUMSTANCES

Writing as Roderic Jeffries

AN AIR OF MURDER
DEFINITELY DECEASED
AN INSTINCTIVE SOLUTION
AN INTRIGUING MURDER
MURDER DELAYED
MURDER MAJORCAN STYLE
MURDER NEEDS IMAGINATION
MURDERED BY NATURE
A QUESTION OF MOTIVE
SEEING IS DECEIVING
A SUNNY DISAPPEARANCE
SUN, SEA AND MURDER

DAMNED BY LOGIC

Jeffrey Ashford

This first world edition published 2013
in Great Britain and in the USA by
SEVERN HOUSE PUBLISHERS LTD of
19 Cedar Road, Sutton, Surrey, England, SM2 5DA.

British Library Cataloguing in Publication Data

Ashford, Jeffrey, 1926-
Damned by logic.
1. Suspense fiction.
I. Title
823.9'14-dc23

ISBN-13: 978-0-7278-8279-0 (cased)

Typeset by Palimpsest Book Production Ltd.,
Falkirk, Stirlingshire, Scotland.
Printed and bound in Great Britain by
MPG Books Ltd., Bodmin, Cornwall.

ONE

They sat at a corner table in the small restaurant halfway down Ogden Street. The sharp contrast between their appearances might have caused comment in central London, but here, where styles of living overlapped, it was incorrectly assumed by other customers and the staff that the nature of their relationship was an explanation.

'Will she know what she's carrying?' Piera asked.

'Since she's smart, she'll likely work that out,' Noyes replied.

Piera picked up the bottle of wine and emptied it into his glass, not bothering to halve the contents which remained with his companion. The wine list had been short and lacked any names he recognized, so he had expected his choice to be a *vino de mesa*, but actually it could have earned a respectable number of points from Robert Parker. He drank, replaced the glass on the table. 'You'll meet the *Helios*?'

'If I ain't fishing in Scotland.'

'For you, inadvisable.'

Noyes accepted his rejoinder had bombed. Piera, being a foreigner, lacked any sense of 'humour'.

'You have not yet told me who she is.'

'Melanie Caine. A charlie who'd get a dead man's blood racing.'

'You need to explain.'

You ain't so sharp with the English as you try to make out, Noyes thought, resentfully aware that Piera spoke better English than he did. 'She's on the independent pussy game.'

'And now an explanation of your explanation?'

'She's a prossy good enough that she doesn't need a ponce and can choose her mugs.'

'Then maybe she will wonder about . . .?' He paused for a couple of seconds to remember the phrase. 'About helping herself?'

'You think I'm wearing L-plates. She knows that to

double-time me adds up to her not making any more punters happy.' Noyes allowed a lascivious grimace to dwell on his face as he imagined exactly how he'd act out the punishment he had in mind.

Ansell turned into Bracken Lane. He and Eileen lived in number thirty-four. For most husbands, home at the end of the working day meant a warm welcome, good meal, relaxation, and shared bed. He, however, could expect a sharp, frosty evening and single bed.

He drove into the garage. When car and garage were secured, he went round and into the hall.

'You're late,' Eileen called out from the sitting room.

She was quick to tell him when he did not return at the normal time, which in other relationships could have indicated a wish for an earlier return; in this case, it was a moan. He hung his mackintosh on the Victorian coat stand; the forecast had been for rain, but the sky had remained merely cloudy.

'Did you buy the marmalade?'

He silently swore. 'Sorry.'

His forgetfulness was going to make her even more dissatisfied than he expected. The television was loud enough for him to hear the programme and identify it: *Fifty Reasons for Remaining Single*. A couple in a deteriorating relationship were encouraged to vent their resentments. The audience probably never considered the possibility, however slight, that the pleasure they gained from the raucous discord might in its nature match that which the public had enjoyed at the Roman games.

He entered the sitting room. She briefly looked away from the screen. 'One day, you'll forget where you live.'

Were he feckless, he would already have done so. 'I'll nip down to the corner shop and get some marmalade there.'

'I want a proper brand, not some sort of mush,' she replied without a hint of thanks, instead just more rancour as if he'd already failed on this important mission.

He walked down to the shop in which there was so much stock, stored from the floor almost to the ceiling, it seemed it might offer as much variety as a supermarket. The Pakistani shopkeeper, around his age, produced jars of marmalade of different brands; he chose one, paid for it. They discussed the latest bank scandal and governmental failures before he left and returned home.

He handed her the carefully wrapped jar.

She unwrapped it. 'I far prefer Hero's.'

'He didn't have any.'

'If you'd remembered to buy it on the way back, you could have got what I wanted.'

'And done the owner of the corner shop out of a small contribution to his profits.'

'That's more important?'

'I should imagine so to him.'

'But, of course, not to you.'

'How about a drink?'

'I don't want anything.'

'Yesterday, I bought a couple of bottles of the sherry you like.'

'I said, I don't want anything.'

She liked an evening drink. Did other wives use self-denial as a way of expressing their annoyances? He went through to the pantry and poured himself a strong gin and tonic; hopefully it would provide him with support in the near future.

He returned, sat, raised his glass. 'To health, wealth and long life.'

'Small chance of that when you won't demand a decent wage.'

'In the present financial climate, I doubt anyone presents his employer with a demand.'

'Barbara said only yesterday that our car looks like some old vintage vehicle.'

'I doubt she realizes that they can be quite valuable. I expect she meant veteran.'

'You're always trying to correct someone.'

He drank. On the screen, a husband and wife was each accusing the other of being crude, rude, arrogant, and a liar.

He emptied his glass, decided he needed another drink before he told her. He stood, empty glass in his right hand.

'I'm feeling like having the other half. Are you sure you won't change your mind?'

'Unlike you, I never do. You're drinking too much.'

'This is only the first refill. How much is too much?'

'Do you have to talk when I'm watching?'

He went out, poured himself a second, stronger gin and tonic. Alcohol might be a false shield, but it helped. When he returned, the programme was finishing. At the Roman games, a victim was dragged with hooks out of the arena; here, the husband would continue to suffer.

He drank. He decided the inevitable could no longer be delayed. 'Jack had a word with me this morning. The Rex Cruising Company want us to handle their advertising and launch a new campaign.'

'She's bought herself a new watch,' Eileen said, studiously ignoring her husband's attempt at converstion.

'Who has?'

'Why can't you listen to what I say? Barbara has bought a new watch and naturally hurried here to show it to me. The case is covered in diamonds. I said how lovely, how it suited her, but it'll only make her look even more ostentatious.'

Despite the second drink, he was still reluctant to tell her, but there were no options. He persevered: 'Jack wants a staff member to go on the maiden voyage of the *Helios* to learn about the company and the new boat. He said I'm to go.'

'The company's actually recognized you! So when do we sail? I must know because there'll be so much to get ready. I'll need at least one really nice evening dress and quite a few of my clothes will have to be dry cleaned. I wonder if Barbara would lend me one of her necklaces. I must look as smart as possible.'

'I'm sorry.'

'What about?'

'Only I am going.'

Her expression became bitter. 'I suppose you—'

He interrupted quickly, 'I'd no say in the matter. I'm going because I'll be working for the company.'

'Did you ask for me to go with you?'

'I'm afraid there was no point to doing so.'

'You can enjoy yourself, I have to stay at home and rot?'

'You must know that's not how it is.'

'Isn't it? Did you offer to pay for me?'

'What was the point when we haven't the money. You bought the new curtains and sofa because Babs said—'

'That's right, blame me.'

'I'm not blaming you.'

'You think I never read the cruising advertisements in the papers or listen to them on the telly? Cruises are wonderful for meeting people. The women shown in the adverts are always young, lithe, wearing minimal bikinis. You're hoping to find some woman who'll invite you into bed.'

'Eileen, I'm going on the cruise because it is part of my job. Can you really think that some amorous twenty-year-old is going to throw her arms about me and invite me to pull her pants down?'

He drained his glass. He was slightly surprised that she had scratched with the nails of a cat, not the claws of a tigress.

Detective Chief Superintendent Abbotts read the email on the computer screen in front of him and, with a sigh of exasperation, looked up at the man standing in front of him. 'This suffers from more possibles than a politician's promise. I quote: "Further information suggests mule may collect diamonds on cruise ship *Helios*, which sailed from UK on the fourth of June, from one of the ports on the North African coast. Her name is possibly Melanie Caine, Carne, Crane or Crone."'

Abbotts send the email to print with a decisive click of the mouse and put the resulting sheet of paper down on the desk in front of him. 'And perhaps she will turn out to be a hippy who calls himself Mick . . . Did you see the telly programme about illegal diamond mining in Sierra Leone?' he asked, his thoughts rapidly moving on.

'No, sir,' the detective inspector replied. He was patiently standing in front of his super's desk, waiting for orders, having been summoned into his office just moments before.

'The workforce are virtually slaves.' Abbotts leaned back in his chair. 'Bust the smuggling and maybe some of those poor sods will have the chance to return to freedom. But what's the chance, when the only evidence is at half-cock?'

'I suppose with a bit of luck, it might provide a lead,' the detective answered hopefully.

'Buy a lottery ticket and I might become a millionaire . . . Make what you can of it, will you?' He did not bother to specify what enquiries were to be carried out. Only those whose standards matched his worked under his direct command at county HQ.

The detective inspector made his way down to his office, which was smaller and noticeably less well furnished. He sat down at his own desk and considered what enquiries he should initiate. Contact the company which ran the MV *Helios* and determine if any passenger was named Caine, Crane, Crone or something similar . . . He shook the mouse on his desk to bring his PC back to life and set about writing his first email of many.

There were those who thought the *Helios* beautiful and welcomed the onboard pleasures which made the time spent at sea less boring: the shops in the large atrium; theatrical shows with long-legged dancers; the cinema in which newly released films were shown; deck games and competitions hosted by jolly-hockey-stick crew members; clay pigeon shooting. And, according to the cruise company's website, a whole host of other activities, too numerous to mention.

There were others who remembered when liners were graceful, seaworthy ships, not ill-proportioned, floating hotels which might founder in a force ten gale. But, this particular ship was almost completely full to capacity, so the shareholders were certainly not complaining about the profits that were being made on this cruise.

MV *Helios* was a day's steaming from Gibraltar when the public address system announced that in about an hour, they would sight a windjammer, a view rarely enjoyed, even by those fortunate enough to sail regularly with the Rex Cruising Company.

Ansell, along with most of the other passengers, stood by the starboard rails on the boat deck – boats were swung inboard two decks below, tradition dictated the name.

Someone came and stood beside him.

'Is she in sight yet?' the newcomer asked.

'I can't see it.'

'She, not it.'

He turned to face a woman in her twenties. Not catwalk, haughtily beautiful, but second-glance attractive. Blonde, wavy hair, long in the current fashion, dark brown eyes, shapely eyelashes, retroussé nose, flawless skin, generous, welcoming lips. Her colourful dress discreetly indicated a shapely body.

'I wonder how close to . . . her we'll get,' he answered, a smile playing on his lips, surprised that this young woman was being so friendly to him.

'Steam close.'

Her corrections amused him. 'Steam in a motor vessel?'

'You would motor towards her?'

A feisty woman.

'We'll keep to leeward of her in order not to steal her wind, so we'll probably be reasonably close,' she continued knowingly.

'You sound seamanlike.'

'My brother had a six-metre dinghy and bullied me into crewing her.'

'You didn't enjoy it?'

'When it was sunny and there was only a moderate breeze, it was fun. But, a strong wind, a choppy sea, my brother imagining himself rounding The Horn, me wet to the skin, the fun suddenly palled.'

'Suffering is said to be half the pleasure of sailing.'

'You've obviously done very little.'

'None at all,' he admitted.

'Try it and learn how much pleasure the suffering gives you . . . Do you know how long we'll be in Gibraltar?'

'Half a day.'

'And in Palma?'

'I'm not certain.'

'I'm wondering if it'll be worth landing there.' It almost sounded like an invitation to spend the time with her. Ansell dismissed the possibility.

'Depends on your tastes. If you like a mixture of the new

and the old, quality and quantity, a market which offers fish whose authenticity it's difficult to accept, it is.'

'You obviously know the place?'

'I lived in a village outside Palma for quite a time.'

There was another announcement from the loudspeakers. 'The windjammer is now just visible five degrees on the port bow. We will be abeam of her in just under fifteen minutes.'

As did almost all the other passengers, he stared out to port.

'You're being too impatient,' she said. 'She'll be visible from the bridge quite some time before down here.'

'How is a landlubber to know that?'

'I won't comment in case I offend you.'

There were excited voices as a smudge on the horizon became masts, sails, hull. *Helios* altered course to close.

'A four-masted barque,' she said, as she used a hand to shade her eyes from the sun.

'Barque? When they said windjammer, I thought she'd be a full-size sailing boat.'

'Ship. A barque isn't named from her size, but her sails. Square-rigged for'd, fore-and-aft at the stern. She's maybe three thousand tons.'

They drew abeam; passengers waved, a greeting poorly returned, perhaps because of contempt for those who sailed in luxury. As the minutes passed, the hull, the sails, and finally the mastheads slipped below the horizon.

'How my brother would have liked to see her,' she said.

'You have no video camera, essential equipment for a tourist?'

'I've never taken a film which hasn't been out of focus.'

He looked at his watch. 'May I offer you a drink?' he ventured. She was still being friendly, so what did he have to lose?

'With pleasure.'

They walked aft to the Bar Orpheus which provided a semicircular view of sky and sea, the latter split by their wake.

'What would you like?' he asked, as they sat at one of the tables.

'A daiquiri, please.'

'I'll join you.' He called the bar steward over and gave the order.

There were two small china bowls on the table; cocktail biscuits were in one, peanuts in the other. She chose a biscuit, nibbled. 'Did you live for long near Palma?'

'For something over six months.'

'Recently?'

'A few years ago. When I was young enough to believe that a good degree in English would enable me to write a novel which would have the critics thumbing through Roget's *Thesaurus* for ever more words of praise.'

'And it didn't or they didn't?'

'Publishers aren't as thick as writers like to believe them to be. The script was regularly returned until I accepted it was unpublishable.'

'So then?'

'I presumed I wouldn't enjoy starving and should find a job. Having a slight facility with words and accepting that the more absurd the claim, the more readily it will be received, I went into public relations.'

'Something you still do?'

'That I'm doing now.'

'On a Mediterranean cruise?'

'My firm has the Rex Cruising Company on its books. I was told to project an advertising campaign which would wow the stay-at-homes. I was provided with a berth to heighten my appreciation of the wonderful pleasures the company's ships offered: the advantage of one-class only, the chance to enjoy new, long-lasting friendships, the haute cuisine meals . . . And so on.'

'You find that an easy task?'

'Not too difficult since I have a fertile imagination and a talent for hypocrisy.'

The bar steward brought them their drinks, apologized for the time taken due to the need to draw more limes from Stores.

Ansell raised his glass. 'To health, happiness, and wealth.'

'It's absurd!'

'Which of the last two?'

'We're chatting away and don't know each other's names.'

'Easily overcome. David Ansell, twenty-eight, married.'

'Melanie Caine, slightly over twenty-one, divorced.'

'Let's drink to Melanie and David on their introduction.' He raised his glass and met her eyes as she too joined her glass to his.

They drank. She put down her glass. 'Is your wife aboard?'

'At home.'

'She dislikes the sea?'

'My company watches the cents, so I was provided with one bunk in a double cabin.'

There was another public announcement. 'Tonight, there will be a dance, beginning at twenty-two hundred hours. For those who have not yet gained their sea-legs, that is ten o'clock this evening. We hope the girls will wear their most gorgeous gowns and there will be an award to the wearer of the one that the judges most admire. Bruce and Hazel who, you will remember, appeared in *Strictly Come Dancing*, will be giving an exhibition of the tango and samba so you'll learn how to wiggle seductively. Later, they will judge which couple are the best dancers and the lucky pair will win a special prize.'

'A good P.R. address?' she asked lightly.

'A shambles.'

'Why?'

'The assumption that listeners will not know or be able to work out what time twenty-two hundred hours is; that the mainly elderly passengers can remember how to wiggle.'

She gave a smile and then looked at her watch. 'I'd better go and spruce up for dinner.'

'Are you going to the dance?'

'Probably not. It can be dull if one doesn't know anyone.'

'They'll make it a jolly affair with lots of Paul Joneses.'

'Very unlikely when no one under eighty knows what that is.'

'Then may I offer myself to try to stave off boredom?' Ansell asked tentatively, doubting so young and attractive a woman would want to spend time with him.

She smiled. 'It's a case of, I thought you'd never ask.'

'D'you know what I'd like to do now?' she asked as they waited for the main crush of people to leave the ballroom.

'Soak your feet in warm, soft water.'

'You didn't tread on them once. I want to go out on deck and enjoy the beauty of a moonbeam across water.'

They went up to the top deck which provided an unobstructed view of the moonlight across the sea. She linked her arm with his as they reached the after teak handrail.

'Up to expectations?' he asked after a couple of minutes.

'Magical. Who said that to enjoy beauty too long was to lose one's love of the life we lead.'

'I've no idea.'

'You should have if you're going to write the great novel.'

'An ambition buried when I finally decided Dickens wouldn't be getting off his pedestal.'

'I'm feeling tired, David, so I think I'll make for bed.'

'Surely bunk?'

She laughed, squeezed his arm, released hers. 'My task now is to navigate my way down to my cabin amidst the maze of alleyways and cross-alleyways.'

They went below to E deck and cabin thirty-five. She unlocked the door. 'I'm lucky and have this to myself. The intended cabin companion fell ill so her misfortune became my fortune. So much more comfortable to be on my own.'

Without conscious thought and to his annoyance, a question slipped into his mind.

Was she merely expressing the average person's reluctance to share sleeping space with a stranger? When the band had played old-fashioned music to please the majority of passengers, she had nestled against him and he had become aware of the swell of her breasts and the brush of her thighs.

'Sweet dreams, Taffy.'

'Taffy?'

She smiled, went into the cabin, closed the door.

TWO

They were thirty-six hours in Naples. Melanie demanded they be proper tourists and join the tour of Pompeii even though their guide would be the redhead crew member whose jokes they found to be even more dismal than those of others in Entertainment.

After a time viewing the ruins, the guide brought them to a halt. 'As I explained earlier, we are now in a semi-restricted area. Are any of you ladies under age?'

There were a few giggles.

On the first villa they entered, there were explicit murals on one wall. Most women allowed themselves disapproving glances, Melanie studied a mural depicting couples in various and sometimes complicated positions. 'D'you think the man on the right is double-jointed?' she asked.

When Ansell didn't quickly answer, she turned to face him. 'I've embarrassed you?'

'You mistake surprise for embarrassment.'

'Surprised I asked?'

'That you seem not to know that only a handful of mammals, not including man, have bones in the object in question.'

'I learn something new every day.'

'For once, ignorance might be condoned.'

Melanie laughed. A nearby, elderly woman looked disapprovingly at her. She murmured, 'I've just shocked the old biddy over there. Very improper to be amused by sex.'

'Observed dispassionately, it does offer some of the most amusing moments known to mankind. Chaucer knew that when he wrote *The Miller's Tale*.'

'I've heard that that is pretty risqué.'

'Depends on one's sense of humour.'

'D'you think there'll be a copy in the library?'

'I doubt it. Not to the literary taste of the average cruise passenger.'

'Then you can tell me the story later.'

Her manner intrigued, perplexed, confused him. Her unsubtle interest in sex could indicate to an active mind that an advance would not be rejected. Yet when he saw her down to her cabin at night, he was dismissed. In schoolboy terms, was she actually just a prick-tease?

The lights of Naples merged into a glow and dimmed into extinction. One of the latest, highly praised films was shown in the cinema after dinner that night.

'Why do they make such gloomy films?' she asked, as they walked out of the cinema after most other viewers had left.

'Truer to life. What would you like now?'

They walked arm-in-arm along the alleyway, untroubled by the slight movement of the ship.

'I'd like to be cheered up.'

'I'm not very good at telling jokes,' he said. 'I either forget the punchline or mess it up. How about a cheerful drink?'

'Liquor is a depressant.'

'Champagne is a guarantee of carefree fun. Halfway through the first glass, you'll be gay.'

'I hope not.'

'Apologies. I still think of the word in its old sense.'

'You said you were only twenty-eight.'

'Part of me seems to live in the past.'

They went up to Bar Orpheus. The bar steward asked if they would like Moet et Chandon, Mumm, or Veuve Clicquot. Ansell chose the last.

'What are we going to do when we've finished our drinks?' Melanie enquired, possibly with a twinkle in her eye.

'Have another.'

'You want me flat on my back?'

'You leave me tongue-tied.'

She laughed.

Twenty minutes later, the bar steward brought them two more filled glasses. Ansell raised his. 'To us.'

'We drink to ourselves?'

'What happier toast?'

'I hope . . .'

'What?'

'Never mind. When are you going to carry out your promise?'

'What promise?'

'To relate *The Miller's Tale* to me.'

'I said no such thing.'

'It was when we were looking at the Romans having fun.'

'Imagination. In any case, I can't remember how the story goes well enough to remember who does what to whom.'

'A futile excuse.'

'Would I lie to you?'

'Probably. Maybe you were wrong and there is a copy of the tales in the ship's library.'

'When it would replace a Barbara Cartland epic?'

'You scorn love stories?'

'When it is inevitable that they'll end happily.'

'A dislike based on personal experience?'

'Why ask?'

'Over these few days, you've said one or two things which made me wonder.'

He possessed the dated belief that matrimonial problems should remain personal. 'Best not to wonder.'

When they left the bar, they walked along the alleyway to a lift.

'Which deck are you?' he asked as the doors closed.

'You don't remember?'

'Afraid not.'

'E deck. But you do know the number of my cabin?'

'Sorry, no.'

'The man's not interested in cabins,' she told the lift.

The doors opened at E deck.

She took hold of his hand. 'Anyone as unobservant as you needs help.' She led the way out, turned to starboard, came to a halt at cabin thirty-five. She released his hand, unlocked the door. 'Thank you for escorting me.' She kissed him on the lips. 'A verray, parfit gentil knyght!' There was laughter in her eyes.

'You've read *The Canterbury Tales*,' he said accusingly.

'I had to study some of them for exams,' she explained with a smile.

'Including *The Miller's Tale*?'

'Far too entertaining to be made the subject of an exam. I read that in my own time.'

'Why the hell didn't you tell me you knew it?' He assumed the guise of a man made a fool of and looked away.

She kissed him again, now with lips parted. 'As the poor miller learned, the past can be inexplicable.' She went into the cabin, did not shut the door this time.

He stared at her, like a teenager, knowing he was a fool yet wondering, hoping.

'You said it was wrong of me to persuade him to buy you for me, didn't you, Georgie?' she said as she picked up the toy Barbary ape she had persuaded him to buy for her that first day they spent together, on the half-day trip to Gibraltar. She replaced it on the sofa. 'I promise not to persuade him to do anything else,' she said to the toy monkey, with her teasing eye trained on Ansell who was still lingering in the doorway of her cabin.

She unbuttoned her dress, drew it up and over her head, carefully placed it on a hanger. She took off an embroidered slip; she wore no brassiere. She began to lower her embroidered pants, looked up. 'Are you waiting for an engraved invitation?'

THREE

The *Helios* passed through The Pillars of Hercules and turned north. The Bay of Biscay was not rough, but foretold the weather that TV reports suggested was likely to be expected on their arrival in the UK – strengthening cold winds and overcast skies; few passengers chose to remain on the open decks. Waves smacked against the hull and occasionally the spray reached up to render the lower port holes briefly opaque.

Melanie and Ansell continued to enjoy their pre-dinner drinks in Bar Orpheus. The bar steward, judging shipboard romance would make Ansell a generous tipper, was quick to serve them and make certain the small bowls on their table were filled with cocktail biscuits, salted almonds and peanuts.

On this, their last evening, the waiter brought them their orders and, trying to make a final good impression on them – in the hope it would increase his evening's tip – remarked they would probably be glad to hear the sea was not expected to become any rougher that night.

'Are you a good sailor?' Melanie asked Ansell as the bar steward left.

'Normally, yes, until the seagulls make for shore.'

She drank, replaced her glass, picked up two salted almonds, did not immediately put them in her mouth. 'I spent a small fortune in that last shop we went into in Lisbon.'

'I did notice!'

'The quality of the embroidery was so wonderful.'

'I look forward to seeing you wearing them.'

'But will you?'

'Why not?'

'You're married.'

He was silent. There was no comeback to that.

'Have you considered a divorce?'

'No.' He said it in a tone laced with both pain, guilt and anger.

'I'm a fifteen-day entertainment?'

'How can you suggest that?' he demanded. 'I haven't thought about divorce until this trip and since then, for me, all reality has vanished.'

'Your wife will surely bring it back?'

He found it difficult to give an answer which would please either of them. Luckily for Ansell, Melanie didn't feel the need to pursue that train of conversation.

Three hours later, in her cabin, reality became a mural in Pompeii.

He awoke.

'I was beginning to think you should be called Rip van Winkle,' she observed.

After endless years of sleep, Rip van Winkle had awoken to learn his termagant wife had died. Ansell studied Melanie. She sat on a chair at an angle which caused the light from the port to sharpen her profile. A morally destructive, impossibly desirable woman.

'I don't know what to do, Taffy,' she said.

'Come here and I'll show you.'

'Whilst you've been snoring . . .'

'I never snore.'

'Whilst you've been snoring, I've packed and can't get Georgie into either of my cases.'

'Carry him.'

'A dolly at my age?'

'Why do you call him Georgie?'

'After a boyfriend who gave me a fortune.'

'I hate him.'

'You're wasting your spleen. He was six and I was five, the fortune was a sixpenny piece which he said was pure silver. Soon afterwards, his family moved north and I never saw him again. I was heartbroken.'

He laughed.

'You're being cruel.'

'I'm sorry.'

'You're still laughing inside.'

'I'm feeling sorry for the emotional suffering you endured.'

'Liar! Could you find room for Georgie in your case?'

'Only with a real squash.'

'He's very resilient. And you're being very slow. Find room for him and I know I'll see you when you return him to me. Or maybe you won't want to see me again; for you, it's just been light entertainment.'

'You know it's been the most exciting, intoxicating time of my life.'

'But it's still a case of, that's it?'

'Can't you understand?'

'You're in a duff marriage, but at home you're a man of honour. Doesn't matter how desperately I'll want to be with you again, to become so horny I'll explode.'

As for Ansell's home life, and future physical comforts, the coming days, weeks and months were fixed. Eileen had demanded two beds in their bedroom. She would undress and put on night clothes in the bathroom. She would expect him to kiss her goodnight, but her lips would be closed. If he made a mistake – there had been times when experience had been overtaken by desire – she would quickly reinforce experience. Melanie offered an escape from frustration.

He looked at Georgie. 'I'll fit him in, even if I have to discard something.'

In Ansell's cabin, the second occupant, Crowhurst, was on the settee; his speech was alcoholically disturbed. 'Been busy, have you?'

Ansell crossed to his bunk, put Georgie down on it.

'Got to wondering where you was. Reckoned you was enjoying more than what they said the trip would give us.'

Ansell lifted up his suitcase on to the bunk, rearranged the contents.

'Give you that monkey, did she?' Crowhurst asked.

He ignored the question.

'Been like them, at it all day and all night?' his cabin mate said with a lascivious smirk upon his lips.

'Would you like to keep your comments to yourself?' Ansell

finally answered, still busily repacking his bag, not glancing at the man's sneering face, for fear of doing something he might regret.

'Said something to upset you, have I, squire?'

Ansell wedged Georgie into the suitcase, closed the lid, and left the cabin as quickly as he could. He was determined to try and see Melanie again before they disembarked.

The *Helios* had docked and after a relatively short wait, the passengers had begun to leave. Melanie had waited until the last minute in her cabin, making the most of the luxury for as long as it lasted. Then she'd prepared herself for disembarking, making sure that there was no way she would bump into Ansell leaving at the same time. However, that was unlikely considering the different exits they were to be using as inhabitants of different ends of the ship.

As her last foot left the gangway and landed on solid ground, she was approached by two uniformed men and calmly, yet forcibly, directed across the quayside towards a large official looking shed. A man stepped forward and introduced himself. 'DC Keene,' he proclaimed and showed her his warrant card.

'What's this all about?' she asked sharply, looking behind her at the crowds of other passengers disembarking behind her. She was relieved to see that no one seemed interested in her being picked out from the crowd and escorted elsewhere. In fact, it was more acceptable these days, to be pounced upon at Customs and Immigration, since 9/11 and the heightened paranoia about security every official had felt since then.

'There is reason to believe, Miss Caine, that you are attempting to bring forbidden items into this country. If you will please cross to that door.' He pointed.

She did not move. 'What the hell . . .?' Her face felt suddenly flushed as fear caused her blood rate to increase.

'Straight to that door.' He picked up her two suitcases.

She hesitated.

'It'll be easier if you do as asked.' The threat was barely cloaked in official politeness.

She began to walk.

They went into an oblong room in which a second officer, Ratner, waited. The window was small, but overhead lights provided sharp illumination. The only furnishings were a long table, a small desk and two benches. Keene put the suitcases on the table. 'Put your handbag down here, please.'

'Why?'

'I wish to search it.'

'Like hell you'll do that.'

Ratner moved closer to her.

'D'you expect to find it full of coke?' she asked sarcastically. Perhaps it was foolish to be acting so belligerently, but she resented their attitude and being made to feel so nervous.

'There may be illegally procured, uncut diamonds in it.'

'Do I look like diamonds are my best friend?' Melanie knew it was a mistake to continue to be antagonistic, but couldn't help herself.

'Do you deny you are in possession of any diamonds?'

'The only diamond I have, cut or uncut, is in the ring I'm wearing. And if you're wondering where I got it, it was a gift.'

'May I have your permission to examine the contents of your handbag?'

'No.'

'The reason for your refusal?'

'I don't like someone messing around with my things.'

'Are your cases locked?'

'Yes.'

'Will you give my colleague the keys, please.'

'Didn't you understand what I've just said?'

'The request was a courtesy, not a necessity. Are the keys in your handbag?'

She did not answer.

Keene opened the handbag and carefully took out the contents, laying each item deliberately on the counter top beside him. He eventually brought out a small set of keys which he handed to Ratner before he then began the task of laboriously replacing all the items back into the bag. Ratner, meanwhile, unlocked the suitcases, and quickly and efficiently examined the contents of the first.

'Does it give you a thrill to feel my pants?' she asked.

He checked the second suitcase studiously ignoring her comment.

'It seems you haven't found the famous Koh-i-Noor,' she said sarcastically. 'Maybe you think I've swallowed it?'

Keene used a mobile to speak to someone. Moments later, a female customs officer entered and crossed the floor to stand by Melanie.

'Miss Owen will conduct a personal search of you, Miss Caine,' he said.

'Like hell she will!' Was this in punishment for her facetious comment about her knickers or swallowing the diamond?

'You will find it much more comfortable to accept the fact. A forcible search can be disturbing.'

'Do as you say or get beaten up?'

'Come on, Miss Caine, don't make it more difficult for yourself.'

She finally accompanied Owen to the far doorway and went through into a small private room. Ratner finished repacking the suitcases, locked them, handed the keys to Keene who replaced them in the handbag. They sat on the bench.

'It's beginning to look as if she's clean,' Ratner observed, as quietly as he could.

'It's surprising what she could have inside.' Keene sounded hopeful.

'Let's hope it is or there'll be a number of bad tempers around.'

They discussed football and, supporting different teams, argued.

Ansell looked at his watch yet again. He accepted he must have missed Melanie. She had warned him that it was unlikely they'd meet on the quayside given that there were so many passengers milling around. Well, no matter; he had to get home anyway.

On the way to the station, he questioned how soon he could expect to see her again, how long before he could tell Eileen he would be away for a day or two. Since work frequently meant he was away from home, she would have no reason to be surprised.

Did I once promise to honour and obey and to love no other, he wondered bitterly?

Irene Owen came through from the small room, shut the door behind her, and frowning, came up to the bench.

'What luck?' Keene asked.

'Not as much as a sparkle.'

'X-ray?'

'Clear.'

He swore.

'There's nothing in the luggage?'

'No.'

'Then you've been given a bum deal.'

'Carry on and remind me I've got a mortgage I can't afford and the house is on negative value.'

'No need to take it out on me. I just do what I'm told.'

Further conversation ceased when Melanie, having dressed and made herself as presentable as she could in the circumstances, came up to the bench. She faced Ratner, her anger and resentment obvious. She slurred her words. 'That was humiliating.'

'If we have cause to strip-search a disembarking passenger, we are legally entitled to do so.'

'And she wanted a thrill.' She pointed at the female officer.

'You have no right to make so obnoxious and unwarranted an accusation,' Officer Owen retorted with as much dignity as she could muster in the circumstances.

'After what she did to me, I was being bloody polite.'

'You are free to leave.'

She set the suitcases on the trolley, slung the handbag over her shoulder, and left. As she crossed the remaining ground of the forecourt, she was relieved to see that all the ship's passengers had since left and there was no sign of a lovesick Ansell waiting around for her. It would have been further humiliation to have to describe to him the reason for her delay.

No other passenger ship was expected for two days. The

driver of the one remaining taxi prepared to accept her fare, swore when she crossed to a waiting luxury saloon car.

A man got out of the saloon, took the two suitcases from her.

'Well?' Noyes asked as she got into the back of the car.

'No problems,' she answered.

FOUR

Bracken Lane belied its name; not one frond of bracken grew in any of the small front and much larger back gardens; in fact the lane was a suburban road. The houses on both sides had been built in the early twentieth century for those with moderate to fairly good incomes. In estate jargon, they offered quality living.

It was here that a taxi deposited Ansell after his two weeks away. He climbed out of the car, paid the taxi driver, carried his suitcases to the front door, unlocked it and stepped into the hall.

Almost immediately, Eileen came out of the sitting room. 'You're late.'

'There was some sort of foul-up over tugs, so we didn't land when we were meant to.' He went forward to kiss her; she offered her cheek.

'I've tried to keep the meal warm.'

'How are you, sweet?'

'The same.'

Discontented. 'Have there been any problems?'

'Jane lost her baby three days ago.'

'Oh, what bad luck!' he said with genuine feeling.

'It was her own fault. I told her, she shouldn't keep rushing around looking after Jim.'

Ansell nodded in agreement, then escaped and went up to their bedroom, put the suitcase down on his bed, opened it. He brought out Georgie, slightly crumpled, and put him down by the case. Melanie had said she couldn't give him an address or telephone number until she decided where to stay, but she'd ring him as soon as possible. It seemed likely she would have a mobile, so why hadn't she given him the number of that as she'd told him her life would be very grey until she was next with him? He was already thinking about her and now that he had landed back to reality with a jolt, he found himself questioning the validity of their relationship. No, he must stop that, he chided himself. All would work out and she would get in touch when she could. Meanwhile, back to reality.

'Are you coming down?' Eileen called out impatiently.

'On my way.' He brought his present out of the suitcase. An attractive, tooled-leather handbag, in a pink coloured box – her favourite colour.

He went downstairs and into the kitchen. 'A little something, dear, to make up for your being left on your own.'

She unwrapped the handbag, examined its interior. 'It's a pity there aren't more compartments for all the things I have to carry. The meal's in the oven, apple pie is in the fridge.'

He ate in the dining room. There was room in the kitchen for a corner table and two chairs and he would have set them up, but 'they' ate in the kitchen, 'we' do not.

The front doorbell rang. He heard the newcomer talking to Eileen, but had to guess who she was because the kitchen door had swung shut. Judy – fun but condemned for flirting with other husbands; Gertrude – her looks suited her name; Yvette – a keen member of the local dramatic society, not nearly as good as she thought herself. He helped himself to a second portion of apple pie, poured over it more cream than Eileen would have approved.

'David,' she called out, 'come on in and say hullo to Babs.'

Barbara – avid collector of gossip, preferably defamatory in nature.

He finished eating, went through to the drawing room, as Eileen liked it to be called. He would have considered Barbara attractive – in appearance – had she not used so much make-up and dressed for effect.

'Just back from your cruise, then,' Barbara said, stating the obvious as if it was an unexpected surprise. She came forward for a cheek kiss-kiss. 'Did you enjoy it?'

'Parts more than others.'

'Babs is booked on a cruise to the West Indies,' Eileen said.

'One of the few places left which still has some class,' Barbara observed.

The two discussed the new shop which had opened in the High Street. Barbara judged the dresses as of very medium quality, but, of course, one had to spend in order to be elegant.

She proved there was no connection between cost and elegance, he thought.

Eileen said she'd bought a very pretty blouse at the established dress shop in Market Road and Barbara must see it.

'I simply haven't the time. I'm meant to be giving Teresa help with organizing an appeal in aid of something-or-other.'

'It won't take five minutes.'

As he heard them going upstairs, he recalled the afternoon in Madeira when Melanie had bought two – or was it three – embroidered blouses.

When they returned, he stood. One of his few habits to gain Eileen's approval was his manners, installed by parents who had held that times might change, respect for others did not.

'What a strange looking monkey,' Babs said.

'Sorry?'

'Where has your mind just been? The monkey on your bed. I've never thought you to be the kind of man who buys mementoes of trips. They're always so mundane and badly made.'

'He has no taste,' Eileen said hostilely.

'Does any husband? I really must get a move on or Teresa will think I can't be bothered to help. Goodbye, David.'

Cheek kiss-kisses.

They chatted at the front door before Eileen returned to the drawing room. 'What the hell's been going on?' she demanded.

'What's the matter?'

Her voice rose. 'Don't try to make out you don't know. D'you think I'm blind?'

'Depends if you want to see what you're looking at.'

'The usual "smart" remark.'

'If you would only explain what's upset you?'

'You damn well know it's that monkey.'

He remembered he'd left Georgie on his bed. 'Barbary ape, actually.'

'Who gave it to you?'

'I bought it.'

'Babs is right.'

'Makes a change.'

'You've been away umpteen times and never before brought

back tourist trash. Some woman gave it to you. It stinks of cheap scent and there are blonde hairs caught up in the fur.'

He stilled the sudden panic. 'Can't think why that worries you. The woman who sold me the ape had blonde hair and smelled as if drenched in something.'

'I know you're lying.'

'Then there's small point in my repeating the truth.'

'You made me look a fool. When I took Babs up to the bedroom, she had to poke her nose into everything. She picked the monkey up, smelled the cheap scent, saw the hairs, said you'd been having a very energetic cruise. Now she'll tell everyone you had an affair with some slut on the boat. What are my friends going to think?'

'They'll believe her and smile knowingly.'

Eileen stormed off. She went upstairs. A door was slammed shut. It was, he thought, her character to be more worried about what people would think than the actual act of his adultery. But she would not demand a divorce. To be divorced could give friends the opportunity to say it was her fault.

FIVE

'Piera is going to shout,' Noyes said angrily. 'You took a goddamn risk.' They were in the car still, negotiating traffic into the city.

'I didn't have any alternative,' Melanie countered. 'I was sussed when I was given the sparklers.'

'How d'you know?'

'Come on, Steve, we can both name a man a split, even if he's had a bath.'

He muttered an acceptance of what she said. There was very often something – too sharp an interest, too marked a disinterest, repeated sightings – which identified a policeman to a villain, a villain to a policeman.

'To land them, I had to have someone who looked like he'd never lifted a bar of chocolate. And it's a bloody good job I did pass 'em on. They tore my luggage apart and strip-searched me.'

'Who's got them now?'

'He does – Ansell.'

'Didn't he want to know why he was taking the monkey through?'

'He'd got beyond asking anything except for me to get 'em off. It's a Barbary ape.'

'I don't give a shit if it's King Kong.'

His temper was always on a short fuse. She introduced a touch of humour to try to defuse it. 'Then King Kong would have been carried by Georgie and the law would have been very interested in him.'

'How d'you persuade him?'

'Diamond sex. Then said my suitcases were filled to bursting because of all I'd bought in the places we went to together and I couldn't pack Georgie.'

'Anyone with half a brain would have wondered if you were getting him to run something black through.'

'His brain was still in bed with me.'

'He wasn't fingered?'

'I told you, he'd have given himself away if he'd been carrying as much as an extra pack of cigarettes.'

'How d'you plan on getting it back?'

'"It"? Poor Georgie? If he could hear you, he'd be very hurt.'

This time, her light teasing annoyed him. 'How?' he demanded angrily, smacking the steering wheel of the car with the palm of his hand as he drove.

She hurriedly answered. Noyes had the appearance of a Mr Anybody, but few equalled his capacity for violence. 'I phone David and tell him where to meet me to return Georgie.'

'What if he doesn't?'

'He'd cross the Thames on hands and knees to be with me again.'

Noyes momentarily gripped the steering wheel with unnecessary, even dangerous, force as he tried to control his anger. Why the sodding hell couldn't the bitch have found a way of smuggling the diamonds without losing possession of them?

'You phone him where?'

'He gave me his number.'

'Then phone him.'

'Best to hear what Piera wants first.'

Piera's nationality was not easily judged. Black, tight, curly hair, darkish complexion and his mannered dressing tended to deny an English background, but provided no definite suggestion. He had been born in Magburaka, Sierra Leone, to the east of Freetown. Noyes himself used brutality as a way of getting what he wanted, but although he would never have admitted it, Piera frightened him. Having driven Melanie to the house, he was glad to leave immediately.

Once in the dark, comfortless room, with just a desk and chair, computer, telephone and large plasma screen TV adorning the wall, Piera demanded to know how Melanie would retrieve the ape.

'I phone and arrange for him to meet me and hand Georgie over.'

'Phone.'

'But . . .'

'Goddamn well phone.'

'Sure, it's just I want to explain that what I say to him may sound a bit odd because his wife's a bitch and if she answers I have to say I'm calling from his office. And today is—'

'D'you need persuading?' he shouted.

'For God's sake, take it easy. Today's Saturday. The office won't be working over the weekend so if the wife answers, my saying I'm ringing from the office won't sound so bright. I'll get on to him on Monday.'

'You're beginning to bloody worry me.'

'Why?'

'Too many answers.'

'I don't understand.'

'Phone.'

'All right, all right. I'll have to get hold of the number from my bag.'

He said nothing as she left. She went into the hallway, upstairs, brought out of her handbag the square of paper on which Ansell had written his home and mobile phone numbers.

The phone was on a small, battered table to the right of the computer. Conscious Piera was suspicious, that his suspicion could very quickly cause him to become violent, her worry shaded into fear. She began to dial, pressed the wrong key because of nervousness, cancelled the call, redialled.

'Yes?' a woman answered.

She thought quickly. 'It's Helen, Mrs Ansell.'

'Who?'

'Helen Taggart. I work in the same department as your husband. I'm having to prepare an idea to present to the project director tomorrow and—'

'Tomorrow's Sunday.'

'I know that this is very unusual, but the board are meeting in the morning. Frankly, it seems to be a bit of a shambles, especially as it leaves me having to spend much of the weekend at work. So if I may have a quick word with David . . .?'

'He's gone out.'

'Do you know when he'll be back?'

'No, but I don't suppose he will be long.'

'I'll ring again.'

'If you must.'

She replaced the receiver.

'Well?' Piera demanded roughly.

'He's not at home.'

'If you're trying to—'

'I'm not trying anything. The wife said he won't be long so I'll ring back in a bit.'

'You'd better be lucky the next time.'

She mentally shivered.

Half an hour later, she dialled again.

'Yes,' Ansell said.

'Thank God, David! You've got to—'

He interrupted. 'What's the problem, Helen?' he asked, maintaining the cover in case Eileen came out of the drawing room and overheard him.

'You've got to get Georgie to me, fast!'

Eileen did come out. She crossed to the stairs, began to climb them, came to a halt and looked at him. He hurriedly said, 'What exactly is Lomas demanding?'

She resumed climbing.

'For Christ's sake, I've got to meet up with you – soon!' Melanie said, her voice shrill.

Their separation had been brief, but desire made him stupidly believe she was longing for him as much as he was for her. 'Hang on a sec and I'll check where I put it.'

He went up to their bedroom. He'd wanted an excuse to check that Eileen wasn't lingering in the doorway to their room, overhearing his conversation and picking up on every nuance in his voice as he tried to contain his excitement at hearing Melanie's voice and anticipating seeing her again.

Georgie was not on the bed by the side of his unpacked suitcase. Eileen sat in front of her dressing table.

He said, 'They want the ape for the latest publicity stunt. I left it on my bed. Where is it now?'

'While you were out, I burned it.'

As he stared at her, he ridiculously tried to believe she was joking.

'And I'll burn anything else of hers you've got.'

He returned downstairs, picked up the receiver. 'Listen—'

'The bookstall, Charing Cross Station in two hours' time,' she demanded.

'I won't be able to bring it to the board meeting,' he admitted, carrying on with the pretence that the monkey was such an important factor in that meeting, but really believing this was just her excuse to get to see him again.

'You've got to,' she cried, the panic now evident in her voice.

'My wife's burned him,' Ansell admitted, confused by her evident fear and the importance she seemed to be placing on the ape.

Melanie looked up from the phone at Piera, her face etched with fear. He crossed to where she stood, grabbed the receiver out of her hands and slammed it down.

'It'll be all right, Piera,' she said shrilly.

He hit her; she fell backwards against a small table, then on to the floor. 'He's found the diamonds,' he said, stating a fact, not asking a question.

'He doesn't know anything about them.'

He kicked her.

'I swear it's not like you think.' She struggled to find words which would calm his anger.

He spoke slowly, his voice rising until he was shouting. 'You couldn't bring the sparklers through because you reckoned you'd been sussed. To prove that was right, you say they turned your luggage and you upside down looking for them. Crap! You and your man worked out how to lift them and take off.'

'You must believe me. They did turn me over. If I'd had one diamond on me, they'd have found it. The diamonds got through because they were in the monkey he carried. But the bitch has burned it—'

'Diamonds don't burn, you silly bitch!' He stamped on her hand and she screamed. 'Where are they?' he demanded again, his foot raised for another stamp.

She spoke even more frantically. 'He never knew there were diamonds in Georgie. If he had, they'd have nailed him on the spot because he's real straight and would have been so shit-scared. It's that wife . . .'

'You have a lovely body. Don't want it to be spoiled, do you?' He brought a knife out of the sheath on the back of his belt.

She tried once again to make him understand she was telling the truth. He ripped open her blouse, held the blade of the knife against her left nipple.

SIX

In Charing Cross station, Ansell continued to search for Melanie amongst the ever-changing crowd. He looked at his watch yet again and confirmed what he already knew; he had been waiting almost an hour. It was unfortunate Georgie had been destroyed, but hardly the calamity she had seemed to find it. If he managed to buy her another . . .

To try to calm his mind, he bought an evening newspaper. He read, but took in very little, eventually dumping the paper in a waste bin. He bought a sandwich and cup of coffee from a vending machine. By the time he had eaten and drunk, thrown the cling and plastic cup into the bin on top of the newspaper, he bitterly accepted she was not going to turn up to meet him. He walked towards the platform from which the next train he could catch would depart, but came to a stop several feet from the gates. The thought crowded his mind. Something had prevented her leaving on time, now she would be hurrying to meet him. Were he to go before she arrived, she might believe he did regard those days and nights as no more than 'light entertainment'. So, he vowed to wait just a little bit longer . . .

As he opened the front door of number thirty-four, he heard the full-throated laugh which named Barbara Morley. He entered, shut the door. A man said something: Barbara's husband. A negative man since no one of character would have made the mistake of marrying his wife.

Ansell entered the sitting room, briefcase in hand; necessary on a trip to the office, of course.

'Why are you so late back?' Eileen demanded.

'There was a lot of work to do.' He spoke to Barbara. 'How go things with you?'

Her reply was typical. 'Same as always when Tom's not too tired.'

Tom might not have heard. It was difficult to judge whether he was amused or embarrassed by her crude inferences.

'A long time doing what?' Eileen asked.

'Helen had got into a bit of a muddle.'

'I phoned the office. There was no answer.'

'We must have been working in the end room which doesn't have a phone.'

'Or it was the moment critique?' Barbara asked.

'I've just remembered,' Tom said suddenly.

'What?'

'I have to meet someone in five minutes.' He made to pull himself up from the sofa on which he'd been slumped.

'He can wait.' Barbara turned towards Eileen. 'A meeting at the Old Bull and Bush, I suppose. Drinks twice as much as he should, so he can look into the barmaid's dark brown eyes and see a double bed.'

'Don't be ridiculous,' Tom protested but he sank back down into the sofa, resigned to waiting until his wife gave him permission to leave.

They left fifteen minutes later. Ansell went into the hall, opened the front door and tried to conceal his eagerness for their departure.

Tom briefly stopped. 'Good luck, David, you'll maybe need lots of it.' He followed his wife.

Ansell watched them get into their bright red Audi sports car which Barbara often hypocritically disparaged in order to draw attention to the fact they could afford it.

He shut the front door. When he turned round, Eileen was standing in the sitting-room doorway.

'Liar!' she said fiercely.

'Now what?'

'You never met Helen at the office to do some work.'

'If you look in my briefcase, you'll find the papers.'

'Put there before you left here. You were with that woman.'

'Which one?'

'She needs identifying? The woman on the boat who put cheap scent over the monkey's fur.'

'I've only seen Helen.'

'You think I'll believe a lie if you repeat it often enough?'

At Natchfield Farm, a herd of Friesians were driven into their holding paddock. In the shadow of Crastbury Hill, a man refilled the feed trays of the hens he hoped, with little reason, would make him a commensurate income despite the unnecessary import of eggs from the Continent which had been produced in conditions illegal in the UK. In Sudely Woods, the head keeper made his way around the release pen, looking for signs to tell him a predator had been present. He walked up a ride. A hundred yards along, two cock and one hen pheasant rose in a flutter of wings. They cleared the trees and flew towards the large kale field beyond which, in winter, would be good holding ground.

At the end of the ride, he turned into another. Within twenty yards of the road, he noticed newly disturbed brambles to his left. Local and not-so-local young couples favoured the woods during the summer evenings and nights and left visible evidence of their enjoyment on the ground. Dirty young scrubbers, his wife called the females; lucky young sods was his description of the males. Close to the disturbance he saw something which intrigued him until he identified it as the naked body of a woman who had seemingly been savaged by a wild animal.

SEVEN

The area from the road and around the body had been secured by police tape; following a careful search by SOCOs, four pegs, with numbered plastic labels attached, had been stuck into the ground, marking where something of possible significance had been found or noted. Two footprints were being cast with plaster when Detective Inspector Glover escorted the police surgeon, a family doctor who lived near Edlehurst, to the body.

'Hell!' the doctor exclaimed as he gained a clear view of the dead woman.

'It's way beyond the worst I've seen before.' Glover was newly promoted; although lacking neither ability nor self-confidence, he would have preferred to have gained more experience in commanding the divisional CID before having to deal with a murder of this nature.

The doctor put his case down on a patch of dry ground under an oak tree, brought out white paper overclothing, similar to that which the SOCOs wore, and put them on, together with a pair of surgical gloves.

He walked up to the body, visually studied it, physically examined it. One SOCO recorded his moves on a camcorder; a professional photographer worked to instructions. The doctor spoke into a hand-held tape recorder. His judgement: the wounds had probably been inflicted with a double-edged knife; none of the wounds could have been self-inflicted (a fact that was obvious, but had to be recorded); she had suffered heavy battering to the right side of her body; her face was heavily bruised; three fingers on her right hand had been fractured. He recorded the temperature of the body with a forensic thermometer.

He briefly remained standing as he gazed down at the dead woman. The post-mortem should decide whether she had suffered the violence during sexual assault, but his judgement was that the nature of the wounds indicated torture rather than frenzy.

The doctor returned to where Glover was talking to a SOCO. Glover cut short the conversation he had been having, turned. 'What can you tell us, doc?'

'Very little. She suffered heavy bruising and violence to one hand, a knife inflicted the wounds. I'd name it torture rather than straight assault.'

Glover swore. He still found it difficult to appreciate one human could willingly inflict agonizing pain on another.

'Rigor is spreading, but not yet complete, body temperature is fifty-seven. To answer the question you haven't yet asked, death was between seven and ten hours ago – figures as open to error as ever.'

Detective Chief Superintendent Abbotts arrived at Sudely Woods, having driven down from county HQ. He was known among the lower ranks as 'What-if'. Opinions of his subordinates were often met by the question: 'But what if . . .?'

He and Glover watched the pathologist examining the body. 'There's nothing to identify her?' Abbotts asked.

'No, sir. With no clothing and nothing found to help name her, our hope has to be fingerprints.'

'You assume she has a record?'

'Since it seems sex may be ruled out, it's difficult to believe an innocent could suffer such barbaric cruelty.'

'The drug trade?'

'Seems the most likely.'

Eileen had made little attempt to converse that morning before Ansell left to go and buy the paper from the local corner shop. On his return, she continued to read a magazine. Silence had become her weapon of attack and defence.

'Would you like a drink?' he asked.

She might not have heard. He asked again. She shook her head.

As he went through to the larder, he wondered how long it would be before her present resentment dimmed. She still remembered he had laughed at one of the doubtful jokes his best man had made at the wedding party.

He returned, sat. 'Shall we watch?' He indicated the TV in the corner of the room; any company was better than his present one.

She shrugged her shoulders.

He switched on the rolling news. It was a day for pessimists. Half the world was in turmoil. The news became more local. Politicians were praising and damning the latest government proposal. A crash had closed two westbound lanes on the M25. Talks between union officials and arbitrators in the chemical industry had failed to reach an agreement. The wife of a millionaire footballer had been caught shoplifting. A woman had been found dead in woods in Kent. To plump out the last report, Detective Chief Superintendent Abbotts was interviewed by a TV camera team. His answers to the questions were brief and uncommunicative.

'We do not yet know who the unfortunate woman was.'

'She had been mutilated, but I am not prepared to say more than that.'

'It is impossible at this stage of the investigation to judge whether the attacker was mentally unbalanced.'

'The motive has not yet been determined.'

'I am unable to confirm or deny that there is evidence of torture. That is all I can say.'

The next item of news was shown.

'Poor woman,' Ansell said. 'Can you imagine her agonized shouts for the cavalry which never arrived?'

Eileen carried on reading as if he wasn't there.

'They haven't identified her so there may be parents with missing daughters or husbands with missing wives, who'll be in hell until the dead woman is identified. Murder does more than kill its victim; close relations and friends are caught up in the mental pain of death. Yet when the victim can't be named, dozens of people may be affected.' He was rambling now, but desperate to get a reaction out of his mute wife.

She finally spoke. 'Are you trying to be clever?'

'I hope not.'

She resumed reading.

The post-mortem began. Individual wounds and bruises on the body were verbally positioned by the pathologist and recorded, measured and photographed.

Lengths of hair, scrapings from under the fingernails, were gathered; samples were taken from the genital area.

Glover, the senior SOCO and forensic scientists were asked if there was anything more they wished to be done. The body was washed where its surfaces had been stained by dirt or blood.

The internal examination began. Glover was not the only man present who, as far as possible, divorced his mind from what was happening. When concluded, the pathologist briefly spoke to Glover. 'Age around twenty-four or five.' He spoke in short, sharp words, as if rushed; a false impression since when working, he was never in a hurry. 'Generally healthy despite being a heavy smoker. Sexually active, but no indication of sexual activity immediately before death.

'I think the best description of what she suffered is death by a thousand cuts. None caused death, all contributed to shock and a loss of blood which proved fatal.'

'Would you judge it to have been sadism or torture?'

'If there is a meaningful difference, torture. Whoever used the knife, chose parts of the body where injury would not be expected to cause a quick death.'

'Was she on drugs?'

'No obvious signs, but you'll have to wait for the laboratory to confirm or deny.'

'Maybe she nicked a load of cash and the dealer caught up with her . . . Is there any contact evidence?'

'Not so much as a stray hair.'

'Then we have no clothes, birth marks, deformities, contact traces or jewellery. A professional dumped her in the woods, leaving only her prints. I wouldn't bet they'll take us anywhere or he'd have hacked the fingers off.'

As if on cue, one of the SOCOs walked to where they stood and showed Glover several forms on each one of which was a finger or thumb print, taken with the customary difficulty from the dead body.

Late Monday morning, his colleague Betterley slapped a folder down on Ansell's desk. 'Message from on high. More zing. Emphasis on luxurious cabins, gourmet feasts, exotic destinations, the opportunity – tinged with sex – to make new friends. And much less on the benefit and pleasure of learning about the lives of peoples in foreign lands . . . Doesn't do to make a prospective passenger think he might learn something.' He left.

Salter, who worked at the other desk in the room, spoke sardonically. 'You must have made the mistake of painting things as they are, not as the punters must be made to believe they will be.' He gave Ansell a sympathetic raise of the eyebrows and promptly went back to whatever facts he was exaggerating for his own press release on a newly opened businessman's hotel in some generic, dull city.

Ansell took a deep breath and turned back to his own copy. He spent another fruitless forty minutes trying to produce a zingier picture of life on a cruise ship, but remembered too much other detail as he did so, detail not normally relevant to the prospective customers of the Rex Cruising Company. *A barque is named for her sails, not her size. Square rigged for'd . . . Are you waiting for an engraved invitation?*

The phone interrupted now bitter memories. 'David?'

His brain, still with the past, traitorously identified Melanie's voice. 'It's you!'

'Why's that surprising?' A suspicious tinge to the voice.

Eileen. 'Oh, sorry, I've been waiting for a call from a client and I thought you were she.' He tried to explain his way out of his sudden outburst, certain that the disappointment in his voice was all too evident.

'I should have expected you to recognize my voice after all these years. I need you to go to the homeware outlet on the outskirts of town and pick up the material I've been waiting to have delivered for weeks. As you may remember, I need it to replace those cushions in our front room.'

'Will do.'

'And we've hardly any butter. You almost finished it and forgot to put it down on the list.'

'One pack?'

'Yes. And this time take the trouble to make certain it's salted.'

'I'll examine the packaging very carefully.'

She rang off.

His colleague Salter said, ‘Are you expecting a client’s phone call or was that domestic cotton wool?’

‘Why ask?’

‘I was born inquisitive.’

‘In spades. It’s lunch time. A half at the local?’ Ansell suggested, the bitter disappointment still evident in his tone.

‘For you, laced with wormwood?’

EIGHT

Glover, seated at his desk, belched. He should not have encouraged the civilian worker in the canteen to place a few more chips on his plate. He looked down at the notes he had written regarding the murdered woman – known facts, conjectured possibilities. The sheet of paper should have accommodated many more words.

The switchboard called him to say the chief superintendent wanted to speak to him; as always, 'detective' had been left out, but he accepted from whom the call would be.

'Any news from DABS or Forensics?' Abbotts asked.

'Nothing on the fingerprints yet, sir.'

'Anything to report?

'Very little, I'm afraid.' Glover did not try to cover the negative aspect of his answer by adding he and his team were following up every possible lead. Abbotts always accepted that those under his command were working at full pitch; had he thought otherwise, one or more persons would have left his team. 'Part of the trouble is that until we have identification, we're working half blind. Initial evidence from people living around the woods indicates nothing unusual was noted on Saturday night – no parked cars in the woods, no one on the road. One elderly woman said she heard screams, but a neighbour says she's three parts away.

'There's been a second search on a broad sweep around where the body was. The only physical find was a pair of woman's pants stuffed down a rabbit hole which had obviously been there quite a time. The keeper says his pheasants are often disturbed by youngsters enjoying themselves and making the most of being out at night.

'There's a small patch of ground between the road and the brambles which for some reason doesn't drain well and there were four footprints of which we took casts – difference in sizes suggests male and female. That's about it, sir.'

'Have you been on to DABS and told them to stir themselves?'

'They know it's priority.'

'Not what I asked.'

'I've found it causes resentment to pressure them, sir, and that means delays rather than acceleration.'

'I'll have a word with Inspector Lamb.'

The resentment would be carefully concealed, Glover thought.

'I'll be with you as soon as possible.'

Ansell drove into the garage. He picked up from the passenger seat the box of truffles he had bought in the hypermarket just outside Frithton. Eileen's favourite sweet. A dog trainer had told him that a bitch, like a woman, responded to bribery.

Eileen was not at home. On the kitchen table was a note, abrupt in form, short of information. 'Babs. Oven.'

He opened the oven door. Fricassée of chicken, for want of a better name. He poured himself a full glass of red wine, went into the sitting room, switched on the television. There were several minutes of an interview with an MP to which he did not bother to listen. He ignored the weather forecast. His glass was empty, so he left to pour himself a second drink. When he returned, a senior policeman in uniform was asking viewers to help identify the victim of a brutal crime whose body had been found in woods near Frithton. She was in her middle twenties, had wavy, blonde hair, dark brown eyes, regular teeth, was five foot nine in height, slim. Would anyone whose daughter, wife, or friend was missing or had not been in contact when she could have been expected to be, had been in that area and not heard from since Saturday, please inform the police at the number now displayed on the screen.

He drank, tried not to wonder where and with whom Melanie was.

Glover was about to leave his room when the external phone rang. He lifted the receiver, identified himself.

'Heathley, sir. We have a definite identification of the deceased from Sudely Woods. Melanie Anne Caine.'

'Why is she on record?'

'Can't answer that right off.'

'Fax me notes on her case if they haven't been thrown away.'

'Yes, sir.' A sigh.

A resentful acknowledgement of his order, Glover acknowledged, and if nothing had been thrown away, a justifiable resentment due to the amount of paperwork probably stuffed inside a folder. However, in Glover's experience, when a year ago he had requested information to be told that it was no longer available, a lot more work would be involved in the long run if there wasn't a nice fat wad of paperwork now for them to go through.

Some time later, a constable entered, handed him many pages of printed information. He read them. About eighteen months ago, Major Belamy, ex-marines, had been attacked by Melanie Caine and suffered slight injury to his right eye, facial scratches, and a blow to his crutch which had resulted in his being in hospital for a few days. He had reported the incident to the police. The day before the preliminary hearing, he had retracted his evidence. It was noted, without extra comment by the investigating officer, that Belamy's wife had unexpectedly returned from a holiday with friends in Italy on the day of the attack.

Glover used the internal phone to call Frick to his room. Frick sat when told to do so. 'I've received a fax which answers one question, sets up another half dozen.' He passed the paperwork across.

Frick read slowly. An efficient sergeant, was Glover's judgement; that was, provided one ignored his all-too-often expressed opinion of admitting women into the police force.

'Find out if she's moved since she gave the address. If she hasn't, SOCO can search the flat. If she was on the game, there'll be a list of clients.'

Glover had given his orders. He was now back to reading something on his computer screen and Frick accepted he'd been discharged.

Back in his room, Frick picked up a pencil and fiddled with it, turning it round between thumb and forefinger. If Melanie Caine had been on the game, there was the probable motive for her violent murder. He used the internal phone to speak to someone in the CID general room, was annoyed to learn that the only occupant was Detective Constable Belinda Draper. There was a small place for women in the police force, according to Frick, and none in the CID. The work could be emotionally scarring and they lacked the mental ability to face such distress.

Belinda entered his office.

'Grab a seat.' He indicated the one chair on the other side of his desk with the wave of an impatient hand.

Frick had been surprised when, a few days after she had joined the unit, he had heard someone remark that she made a man look twice and wonder. He certainly did not look at her and think of bed. She had a pleasant smile, a tuneful voice, a quiet manner; but so did many other women. And in his opinion, she also suffered from the female belief that she was always right, had no hesitation in arguing, and lacked a traditional respect for authority. All in all, just further justification of his conviction that women had no place in the police force, certainly not in CID.

Back to the present and to the case. If she was the only officer he had at his disposal, he guessed he'd have to make do.

'The Sudely Woods victim has been identified,' he said.

'Poor bitch.'

He was annoyed by her 'canteen' expression. Trying to show she was right up there with the men. 'An unfortunate description,' he said and to his annoyance judged he had sounded prim.

'What's named her?' Belinda carried on regardless of Frick's evident apathy.

'She was accused of GBH. An assault on a married man, Major Belamy – ex-marine – in his house.'

'Was she sent down?' She had her notebook out and was scribbling away whilst asking questions. She was diligent, Frick had to admit.

'He retracted his evidence before the preliminary hearing so the case was shot.'

'What made him change his mind?'

'Most likely because his wife returned unexpectedly early from Italy.'

'Was Caine on the game?'

'No firm evidence, but the circumstances indicate the probability.'

'Helping the husband make up for lost opportunities.'

Frick again expressed his disapproval of her comment. Belinda was amused. He was a good sergeant, notably because he was always ready to help or defend any of his team in trouble or wrongly criticized by a senior, but he could also be so out-of-date.

'Ascertain if the Caine woman, prior to her death, was living in the address given in the fax; if so, find out what you can about her. Have a word with Major Belamy – why did she attack him; how did he make contact with her; anything else about her that could be useful.'

'I'll try not to be embarrassed by what the major tells me,' she said lightly.

'I'd prefer to think you might be.'

He lit a cigarette after she had left. His wife Anne's birthday was only a week away and he had yet to decide what present to give her, a problem which worried most husbands, but few wives. He stared at the small, framed photograph of Anne on the desk and although not taken long ago, he saw a woman little changed by the twenty-seven years of their marriage; if he looked in a mirror, he saw a middle-aged man whose hair was disappearing and whose face was quite heavily lined.

Officers on the beat – the few, these days – were sometimes offered sex in exchange for ignoring some minor incident. He had refused every such offer and was proud of the fact, yet uncomfortable that he could experience pride from those refusals. Why did interaction with a modern, young policewoman like DC Draper lead him onto such thoughts? Perhaps he was just getting too old for the job . . .

Belinda turned off the car's engine and stared up at the block of flats which possessed the visual charm of an oblong block of concrete. A countrywoman by birth and upbringing, she had returned to live with her parents in the country after her relationship with her fiancé, Peter, had soured.

She parked on a solid line, crossed the pavement, turned into the building. The entrance hall was divided into two unequal parts. In the first was a board of named call buttons and small post boxes. By flat one, there was still the name tag, M. Caine; by flat two, Mrs D. Greene. She pressed button two.

A female voice, sounding scratchy through the speaker, said, 'Yes?'

'Mrs Greene?'

'If you're a reporter, please go away.'

'I'm Detective Constable Draper and would be grateful if I might have a word with you.'

'The first reporter said he was a policeman and wanted to ask me questions about Melanie Caine because of what had happened. I was so shocked . . . In the end he went away. Then there were all the others. Some of them seemed so . . . callous just wanting to know about her.'

'Do you have a spyhole in your front door?'

'Yes.'

'If you look through it after I ring, I will show you my warrant card which proves I'm a policewoman.'

She was buzzed in the main door, crossed the tiled floor to flat two, rang the bell at the side of the door on the left-hand side and held up her warrant card by the small hole in the door. After some moments, the door was finally opened.

Mrs Greene, in her early eighties, had her left arm in a sling. Her face showed the inevitable damage of age, but it was possible to judge she had once been attractive. 'Please come on in.' Now confident that her visitor was authentic, the old lady was all politeness.

Belinda entered the narrow hallway in which colour came from the roses in a cut-glass bowl on a small table. 'I'm sorry you've been so troubled by the press.'

'There was one in particular who kept ringing and saying he wanted to talk to me about the poor unfortunate woman. He was quite rude when I refused to discuss her or let him in.'

'It must have been very disturbing for you and, unfortunately, now I'm adding to your worries.'

'As my mother used to say, life was never meant to be easy . . . If you will go into that room, I'll make some tea.'

'Please don't bother.'

'It's none and I'm sure you'd like a cup. I'd rather like one myself and it's nice to share it with someone for a change.'

'In truth, I would. Thank you.'

Belinda entered the room Mrs Greene had indicated. The sitting room was lightly furnished. The two easy chairs were grouped in front of a flat screen television, a bookcase was overfilled with books, the painting on the wall opposite depicted an autumn country scene in which the leaves of trees were beginning to fall.

A morning paper was on an occasional table. She sat, opened the paper, skimmed through the report of the murder. There was no mention of the victim's name; Melanie had not been identified until the middle of the morning, hours after that edition of the paper had been printed.

Mrs Greene entered, stood just inside the doorway. 'Will you tell me your name again? I fear I have forgotten.' She spoke in the clipped tones which once were heard much more frequently.

'Belinda Draper.'

'Mine is Jane Greene. Everything is ready on a tray on the table in the kitchen. Would you be kind and bring it in here? I'm afraid it would be rather difficult for me.' She indicated her slinged arm.

'Of course.' She went through to the kitchen, picked up the tray, returned to the sitting room and put it down on a glass-topped table. 'I'll pour, if you'd like?'

'You mustn't wait on me.'

'The least I can do after all the aggravation you've been through.'

The elderly lady sat, relieved at being able to make use of such helpful company. 'A little milk please, and no sugar but two saccharin pills. One of the perils of becoming old.'

'You've a long way to go before you can call yourself that.' Belinda poured out a cup of tea, picked up the plate on which were chocolate digestive biscuits, offered them.

Jane expressed an interest in Belinda's job. Did she like it, did she think it was safe for a woman? Belinda's answers were far sweeter than they would have been had the questions been asked by a man.

Carefully, she guided the conversation on to the subject of Mrs Greene's neighbour.

'I can't say I knew her at all well even though we quite often met coming in or going out of the building and in the nearby supermarket,' Jane said. 'Occasionally she'd ask me into her flat for a drink or I would ask her in for tea.'

'Was she married?' Belinda now had her notepad out again ready to write down anything relevant.

'She never mentioned a husband and did not wear a wedding ring.'

'Did she have a job?'

'She had a friend who ran a dress company and helped her, especially when one of the staff was ill or suddenly left, which seemed to happen often even though Melanie said they were well paid.'

'Then she was quite busy?'

'Must have been since she often was away. She told me the work was hard, but she didn't mind that because it enabled her to have nice clothes. She was always beautifully dressed.'

'Where was the company?'

'I expect she told me, but I'm afraid I can't remember.'

'Did you meet the friend who ran it?'

'I don't think so. No, I'm certain I didn't.'

'Did Melanie have lots of friends?'

After a pause, Jane said, 'It was strange.'

'What was?'

'Melanie was attractive and friendly, but I don't remember ever seeing her with anyone.'

'One would have expected her to have a number of friends. And perhaps many of them male?' Belinda again tried to lead the conversation; often personal opinions were just as useful as facts.

'I know, but I did have the impression . . .'

'That she preferred a quiet life?'

'I'm probably being rather ridiculous.'

'Most unlikely. I'm sure you're a very good judge of people.'

'Well . . . I had the impression that she disliked men, even despised them.'

'Did you wonder why that could be?'

Jane said nothing.

'Did she ever say anything to suggest she was worried about someone or something?'

'No. But I must say that the day she got back from her cruise, I thought she was very nervous. Indeed, I asked her if something was wrong. She told me to mind my own business. I was really surprised. She'd never before been rude like that and I was only trying to help. Still, later she was friendly and showed me a photo of the ship she was on. It didn't look like they did when I was young, but not much does.'

Belinda phoned Glover. 'I've had a chat with Mrs Greene and haven't learned enough to cover the head of a pin.'

'Of course not, when all the fairies are standing on it.'

'Fairies?'

'And they say the intelligence of the average person hasn't been numbed by the box. Get back here as quick as you like and do some work.'

The team of three SOCOs and Glover attracted the brief interest of passing pedestrians as they left the police van and entered Ashcroft Building. Sergeant Cathart brought out a small bunch of skeleton keys which at different times had been taken from arrested housebreakers and at the third attempt unlocked the front door.

The flat was more tidy than the home of most – if not all – of those present. Dresses, of which there were many, hung in plastic dust bags, shoes were on racks, clothing was carefully folded and in drawers, a couple of magazines on a bedside table were squared with the table. There was a large television set, but no DVD and therefore no disks to collect. There was likewise no laptop, PC or tablet. Every paperback in the two small cupboards was examined page by page for insertions, every piece of paper on which was writing was read. Carpets were raised and floorboards examined for a hiding place. In the bathroom, the lavatory cistern was trawled and every bottle and tin in the medicine cupboard opened. In the kitchen, the refrigerator was emptied, the interior of the electric stove checked by torchlight, china and store cupboards examined.

Cathart reported the obvious. 'Nothing, sir.'

Glover fiddled with some coins in his pocket. 'She won't have worked without some form of records, so where in the hell did she keep them?' He answered his own question. 'In her working place. Here, she lived a normal life.' He looked around at the tidy flat, deep in thought. 'The old girl remarked on her apparent lack of friends, notably males . . . Maybe a retired marine major would be of some help.'

NINE

Despite DC Pascall's unwillingness – he and religion were strangers – he would have taken his wife to the church fête had he not been ordered to question Major Belamy instead. That Pam had believed his professed inability to drive her to the fête was an excuse, had – and still did – annoy him. As he passed through the gateway and passed the bordering oaks, he had a clear view of Manor House; the probability that the major was likely to be a wealthy man was confirmed.

He parked level with the end of a well clipped yew hedge. The gravel turning-circle was newly raked. The lightly carved oak front door, under a lead covered canopy, had been striated by time and weather. There was a well polished brass fox's bell-pull. From inside came the flat sound of a bell. A wonder it didn't sound 'Rule Britannia', he thought sourly.

The door was opened with accompanying creaks. A man in white coat and striped trousers said, 'Good morning.'

Pascall 'heard' a question mark in the other's voice. Was he judged to have come to the wrong door? 'Is Major Belamy in?'

'Who is asking?'

'Detective Constable Pascall.'

'You wish to speak to Major Belamy?'

He would have liked to ask if the other thought he might be there to speak to the chief constable. 'Yes.'

'If you come in I will ask Major Belamy if he is available.'

If he thinks he isn't, he'll learn it's the twenty-first century, Pascall decided. He watched the butler cross to one of the panelled doors, knock, go inside. A woman came into the large hall, from another room and with one glance dismissed him as being of any consequence and walked over to the staircase with spiral balusters and carved tread ends. It pleased him to note she had a fat bottom.

The butler returned to the hall. 'Major Belamy will speak

to you in the study.' He then indicated the way with an outstretched arm and disappeared from view.

The study contained leather armchairs, a kneehole desk, filled bookcases; on the walls hung a tattered white ensign, a large photograph of staged rows of the crew seated or standing under the three guns of the after turret on a battleship, and a painting of HMS *Victory*.

Belamy did not stand but stared at Pascall for several seconds before he said, 'Your reason for coming here?'

'I need to have a word with you.' Pascall made a point of omitting any 'sir'.

'For what reason?'

'We are investigating the death of Melanie Caine.'

'That is supposed to be your reason?'

A cool bugger, Pascall thought resentfully. 'We think you knew her.'

'You are mistaken.'

'Not according to our records.'

'I can only presume you are referring to the unfortunate experience when the woman was shown into the house, claiming she had information concerning the poaching that was going on. When I asked her to name the person or persons concerned, she shouted that people who killed for pleasure were perverted and attacked me.'

'You reported the assault to the police then retracted your evidence.'

'Having overcome the injury she inflicted on me, I accepted that, like all the others, she was incapable of comprehending the stupidity of her behaviour, and it would not be fair for her to suffer imprisonment.'

'Did your servants assist you when you were assaulted?'

'None of them was here. I was forced to phone for help.'

'Why were they not here?'

'I had granted them the day off.'

'Why?'

'That does not concern you.' The major began to look uncomfortable.

'Was it because you wanted an empty house when Melanie Caine arrived?'

'The suggestion is slanderous.' The haughtiness was back in his tone, but Pascall judged it was just his defence mechanism going into overdrive for one last go before he had to admit defeat.

'How did you get in touch with her?'

'You have not listened to what I have said?'

'We have determined that she was an upmarket call girl, ready to service a customer in a hotel, at his home or her pied d'amour.'

'I find it very distasteful to hear you speak about such matters. If you are trying to suggest I had some form of relationship with that woman, I will make my objection to so egregious a mistake to the highest authority.'

He tried to sound angrily outraged, but it was easy now to identify the fear underneath his words. Those who portrayed high standards dreaded having their muddied lives exposed. 'I think, major, that with your wife away, you decided to dismiss the staff long enough for you to call Melanie Caine over here. What to me is inexplicable, is why she attacked you so vigorously. Did she object to what you demanded?'

'Your suggestion is contemptible.'

'But no doubt correct. Is your wife here?'

'No concern of yours.'

'That is true. But it is of concern to you because when she returns and finds me here, still trying to get you to answer my questions, she will wonder what's going on. Perhaps you would find it difficult to explain . . .?'

There was a long silence.

'Did Melanie Caine object to the activity you demanded?'

'If . . .'

He repeated the question.

'If I tell you . . .' Again Belamy stopped before completing the sentence.

'I would leave as soon as possible. You telephoned Melanie and ordered her to come here?'

He nodded.

'What was her number?'

'I . . . I can't remember. I don't have it anymore.'

'You expect me to believe that?'

'It is fact. When my friend gave it to me, I wrote it down. But afterwards I tore the paper up because . . .'

Had he been scared his wife might find the paper and ask him whose number it was or was it the need to destroy the evidence of what, now that passion was spent, was a humiliating memory?

'You say your "friend" gave you the phone number. What is his name?'

'I don't remember.'

'You're living in another world,' Pascall said scornfully. This man needed to face up to the consequences of his own actions. 'I want his name,' he repeated.

'He's married and his wife . . . She'd . . .'

'A little common sense on his part and, as with you, his wife will have no reason to learn about her husband's off-duty life.'

After barely a hesitation, Belamy volunteered a name. 'Sheridan.'

'His address?'

'I'll have to look it up.'

'Please do so.'

Belamy left the room. When he returned, he had a filled glass in one hand and a piece of paper in the other. He handed Pascall the name and address.

Pascall pocketed the piece of paper and left the house with barely an acknowledgement. Mission successful but how he hated those bloody arrogant rich people!

The six-mile drive was past fields with many shapes whose boundaries were marked by thorn hedges and were laid down for hay or in which cattle or sheep grazed.

Frackley Grange, a seventeenth-century house which had been extended in the middle of the twentieth century, was in a small village and on one side of the traditional green. Sheridan, middle-aged, overweight, had a fulsome manner. 'Come along in, constable. Is there some sort of problem which brings you here? If there is, I shall be pleased to help you if I can,' he proclaimed in a cheerful tone, clearly clueless as to the policeman's mission.

'Hasn't Major Belamy phoned you?'

'No. Why do you think he might have done?'

'Is your wife here?'

'Away with friends. The natterpack, I call them.'

'Then you can give me Melanie Caine's phone number and address.'

Sheridan's bonhomie manner vanished. 'Who's she?' he asked, trying, and failing, to sound puzzled. Instead he sounded scared and shocked.

'You've not read about her murder?'

'Oh! . . . But you can't think I could have had anything to do with what happened to her?'

'I don't.'

'Then why mention her as if . . .' He stopped.

'As if you'd met her?'

'It's absurd to think I could have done.'

'As absurd as giving Major Belamy the telephone number of a woman you'd never met?'

'Who says I did?'

'He does.'

'I don't believe that.'

'You've forgotten there's no honour amongst adulterers. The name and address, please.'

This man was easier to crack. Ten minutes later, Pascall sat in the car and reread the address. Cloverdean, Alersham. The guv'nor had been right – the flat they'd found so far had been Melanie's off-duty home. He put the paper down on the passenger seat, started the engine, drove off. He accepted his manner when questioning both men had been sharp and aggressive. But that was often necessary when someone thought he was insulated from others by wealth or breeding. And ultimately, it had worked and that was the point of his job after all.

Cloverdean, a brick bungalow in a two-acre field ringed by a semicircle of woods, was fronted by a lawn and flower beds. Sergeant Cathart checked that the outer front and back doors were locked, so he used a skeleton key to open the back one.

The inside of the bungalow made even he express surprise.

On the walls of the larger bedroom hung pornographic photos and drawings and on the ceiling, above the king-sized bed, was a large circular mirror. This was obviously to accommodate Melanie's form of entertaining, but elsewhere the house had been ransacked and had certainly been made unfit for further socializing. The contents of cupboards and drawers had been emptied on to the floor, the mattress ripped open, pillows cut and the feathers strewn everywhere. The other rooms were as chaotic. Chair seats had been torn, books pulled out of a small bookcase, the TV set ripped open as had been the DVD player, empty disk covers and disks thrown around; in the kitchen, the oven had been attacked, jars and bottles littered the floor, many of them broken and their contents forming a sludge; in the dining room, the smashed contents of a display cupboard lay in a heap. A survey of windows and outside doors was made to determine whether entry had been forced or the intruders had been let in. The interior of the lock of the back door, viewed with the aid of a light probe, showed that it had been forced.

Glover arrived shortly before the SOCO team had finished their work. Cathart met him at the front door. 'The place has been turned into a junkyard, sir.'

'Vandals?'

'Could be, but I'd say more likely someone searching for something.'

Glover went inside. Anne frequently called him untidy; the contents of the bungalow would show her what that word really meant. 'Have you recovered any notebooks, phones, computers, anything with addresses or telephone numbers?'

'All that sort of thing has been put on one side for a full examination, but I've made a very brief check and didn't come across anything that looked interesting.'

'Memory sticks or disks?'

'Just lots of CDs and DVDs with their empty cases all over the place.'

He went outside through the back door. Here, there was no garden, only rough grass, recently cut. A quick movement caught his attention and a squirrel ran up the trunk of a tree and disappeared behind the leaves. He began to pace the ground. Vandalism or a search? Vandals were more likely to have left obscene messages or, lacking spray cans, thrown the bottles of jams, chutney, etc at the walls. Chaos would have been similar, but the form of it different. That the computer had been left marked a search for something which wasn't in the form of information. What had Melanie Caine, an upmarket tart, possessed which provoked that search and, it seemed reasonable to surmise, her torture before she was murdered?

The answer – or part of it – to his question was waiting in Glover's office. A note on his desk recorded a call from Interpol. A report had been received from the inspector general of Internal Security in Lebanon. Having learned of the death of the English woman, Melanie Caine, he would advise the English Constabulary that she had been suspected of smuggling illegally mined, uncut diamonds from Sierra Leone, but had managed to escape detection prior to her departure from Beirut on MV *Helios*. The English authorities had been advised before the arrival of the ship, but the suspect had been found not to be in possession of diamonds.

Glover addressed the window. 'Why the hell does it take someone in Lebanon to tell us? Was everyone here fast asleep?'

He left his room, found Frick's was empty, continued on to the general room. That was equally empty. He went over to the noticeboard under which was a movements book, listing the time at which a person had left and why, where she or he had gone.

He turned to leave as Belinda walked in. 'There is one of you around to do some work, then.'

The DI's mood was clear and forbade any droll comment. 'It's been a hectic day, sir.'

'Find out which shipping company runs the *Helios*.' He left.

She sat at her desk, did not immediately do as ordered. Peter had rung home whilst she'd been at work. Her mother was sufficiently old-fashioned to have disliked her moving into Peter's flat before their marriage, yet had been sorry when she had moved out, having decided he could make her daughter a good husband if only . . . Until one lived with him, one could not judge the selfishness of his character. Anyway, she didn't like to hear that he was calling; moving out had meant to signal a new start for her, away from him and his influence. How could she hope to move on if he still rang for a chat – or whatever excuse he liked to give.

The internal phone rang.

'When did she dock?' Glover asked.

It took a moment to banish Peter and relationship issues from her mind and reorganize her thoughts. 'I'm still looking,' Belinda lied as she shook herself out of her reverie. 'I'm afraid there's rather a long list of companies and I can't yet say.'

'Don't waste time.' It was almost as if Glover had a sixth sense and could judge she'd not yet started the job in hand.

'Then I'll ring off.' She did so. Her comment would not have improved the DI's mood, but it didn't hurt any of the men, whatever their rank, to remind them a WPC wasn't to be dismissed as a mere woman. She went on to Google and searched for a list of shipping companies based in the UK which concentrated on cruising. The first one she phoned sailed to the Caribbean. Hot sunshine, blue, calm seas, warm sand drifted into her mind. Peter had bought a flat in Florida and announced that was where they'd spend their holidays. He had not asked her to see the flat before he bought it or if she would like to go there; when she pointed this out, he had been surprised and then annoyed she should expect him to have done so . . .

Forget the past, she told herself. She phoned four companies before a man in the Rex Cruising Company offices told her they ran MV *Helios*. She had docked after a Mediterranean cruise on Thursday.

'Thursday of last week?'

'Obviously,' the rather facetious salesman on the other end of the phone replied. He won't be getting my business anytime soon, Belinda thought to herself and had to refrain from quoting Glover's Law at him: 'If you don't check, there'll be a mistake.'

She went along to Glover's room and reported back to him.

'Good work.'

As she left, she wondered what had lightened his mood.

Men's moods were so often like weather vanes in an indeterminate wind, swinging backwards and forwards.

In the CID general room, she closed down her computer and cleared the top of her desk. Halfway to the door, her phone rang. She debated carrying on through the open doorway, then thought the better of it.

'Get on to Southampton and ask them to question the staff of the *Helios* about Melanie Caine,' Glover ordered as soon as Belinda picked up the receiver. 'Do you have a photo of her to fax them?'

'Yes.'

She sighed as she turned her PC back on and shrugged off her jacket. She texted her mother to say she would be home late.

DC Smaithe braked the car to a halt by the side of the large trailer from which stores were, via a long mobile conveyor, being loaded aboard the *Helios*. He picked up the envelope in which was the faxed photograph of Melanie's head and shoulders, walked over to the gangway and up to the entrance of the deck.

'Crew boarding pass, please,' said the crew member on watch.

'Detective Constable Smaithe.'

'Like to prove it?' He was less polite now that he knew this wasn't a fellow crewman.

Smaithe produced his warrant card. The seaman briefly studied it. 'Has the mate finally cut the Old Man's throat?'

'Wouldn't be my problem if he had. Are the crew aboard?'

'Half of 'em are on leave.'

'For how long?'

'Won't be back until the day before we sail.'

'Shit! . . . Still, I can have a word with those who are aboard. Who'll organize that for me?'

'Better have a word with the purser.'

He was given instructions, but lost his way amongst the complications of decks, alleyways and cross-alleyways, was hot and bothered by the time he reached the large working space in which were three men in uniform, one with white between gold bars of rank on his shoulders.

'What is it this time?' the purser asked mournfully after Smaithe had introduced himself. The lines in his face suggested many years spent listening to groundless complaints from passengers. 'A mother complaining her daughter was seduced by one of the crew?'

'That often happens?' enquired Smaithe, with interest.

'The complaints or the seductions? Depends on warm weather, calm sea and cocktails.' All four men shared a smile at that, DC Smaithe rather wishing he was booked on a cruise.

'I need to find out if any of the crew remembers one of the passengers on the last voyage.'

'Male or female passenger?'

'Female, but no complaining mother. Can you round up crew members so as I can show 'em a photo and ask if anyone recognizes her?'

'Half the hands are away on leave.'

'The bloke on the gangway told me, but I'm an optimist and reckon there's someone here now who can help.'

'What's this in aid of?'

'One of the passengers who was on your last trip has been murdered.'

'Here, are you talking about the poor woman who was sliced up?'

'That's right.'

'Can't be one of our lads . . . but I'll do what I can to get things organized,' the purser offered helpfully and made to dial a number on a nearby phone.

'By the way,' DC Smaithe asked tentatively, 'is there any chance of getting a quick meal?'

'Catering staff might come up with something,' the purser suggested.

'Champagne and caviar for starters?' Smaithe asked with a grin. He was rather enjoying this on-board experience so far; accommodating crew, he thought.

'You'll be lucky if it's sausages and mash. And there's no booze.'

'Doesn't sound like the wonderful life a cruise is supposed to be.'

'It never is.'

* * *

Three hours later, Fred Hellan, one of the bar stewards, entered the cabin in which Smaithe was questioning the staff.

'Grab a seat,' Smaithe said.

Hellan sat.

'Have you been told what I'm after?'

'My mate says you're trying to find out about a woman passenger on the last cruise.'

'That's right. So have a look at this photo and see if she brings back any memories.'

Hellan studied the photo. 'At first look, she doesn't. Her hair's done very different and she looks older in this yet . . . I reckon I saw her.'

'Second impressions can be sound, so tell me about her.'

'Didn't make one look and whistle. Mind you, that's not to say one didn't look. Know your way around and you'd reckon she'd make a bed rock in double quick time. That's why he was around all the time.'

'Who was?' Smaithe looked up from his notebook, pen poised to put a cross by this man's name, along with all the other previous unproductive interviews.

'The guy who was always in a hurry to get her rocking.'

'Any idea who he was?'

'No.'

'A passenger?'

'If he'd been one of the officers on the make, he wouldn't have brought her into the bar.'

'D'you know his name?'

'No.'

'Which cabin was his?'

'No idea.'

'Can you describe him?'

'Not really.'

'Was he tall?'

'Kind of normal, I'd say.'

'Colour of hair?'

'Reckon it was brown. Though now I think about it, maybe it was black.'

'Any unusual features?'

'Here, why you asking? Thought it was her you were interested in.'

'He may help us.'

'You mean, he did her in?'

'Can't say. Was he fat?'

'Like you.'

'Thin. Was he clean-shaven?'

'The kind of bloke who always shaves.'

'Did he have a moustache or beard?'

'No.'

'Were his ears close to the head or more apart?'

'You don't seem to understand,' Hellan said resentfully. 'Passengers drink hard so I'm having to work hard and there ain't time to look at ears.'

'Of course, but sometimes a person has an unusual physical feature which one notices, even if one does not realize that at the time.'

Hellan's expression suggested to Smaithe that he should not complicate matters; Hellan might be expert at judging a passenger's tipping possibilities, but otherwise his mind was not particularly sharp.

'Did he walk normally or with a limp?' Smaithe suggested, trying to spark some kind of recollection.

'Wouldn't know.'

Frithton's CID, Smaithe thought, would probably not be pleased to learn Melanie's partner was of ordinary height, build and appearance.

'Is that all, then? Got to get below to do some checking.' Hallan was obviously bored by this interview and wasn't going to bother taxing his memory any further.

'Sure. Thanks for your help.' DC Smaithe barely looked up from his notebook as he gestured for the man to go.

'Taffy was a nice bloke for a passenger,' he commented as he stood. 'Never bellyached when I couldn't serve quick because of all the others.'

'Who's Taffy?'

'Been asking about him since I got here, ain't you?' Hallan

gave the policeman a confused look before he walked out shaking his head.

Later, Hellan told another crew member that the police were dumber than the old girl sewn up in canvas they'd dropped over the side two voyages back.

TEN

In Belinda's email inbox was, she noticed as she sat down and shook her mouse into life, an urgent email report. She read it. How to use a couple of hundred words to say little of consequence. The description of Melanie's companion on the *Helios*, provided by a crew member, named him Taffy, but that was all.

She went along to the detective inspector's office. 'Re the *Helios*, sir.' She handed Glover the printed out email; he much preferred to hold pages rather than rely on words on a screen.

'They've taken their time.' He read. 'Was the interviewer a cadet with only a month's training?' It was tradition that the staff of other forces were incompetent. 'His name was Taffy. Very relevant! Taffy was a Welshman, Taffy was a thief . . . How does it go on?'

'I don't know.'

'You sound as if I'm offending your political correctness.'

'My father is Welsh.'

'I'll try and think of a derogatory English rhyme to even things up . . . Sergeant Frick is organizing the questioning of people living near Sudely Woods to find out if they can come up with something. You'd best join him.'

She crossed to the door, opened it.

'Didn't Taffy steal a leg of beef?' he called out.

She closed the door behind herself with unnecessary force.

Ansell drove into the forecourt, once a small front garden, parked in front of the garage of number thirty-four. He locked the car, crossed to the front door, stepped inside. Eileen was talking to someone in the sitting room. He identified Helen. An angular woman in body and thought.

He went straight up the stairs to the third bedroom which he used as an office, sat at the desk and began to work on papers he had brought home. He hoped he'd got away with it, but sighed when it turned out he had not.

'David,' Eileen called out. 'Come on down.'

'I've work which has to be finished yesterday,' he called from the top of the landing.

Moments later, having sat back down at his desk, the third tread from the landing squeaked, warning him she would soon be with him. He picked up a ballpoint, moved a sheet of paper in front of himself and starting writing.

She entered. 'Doesn't matter how much work, you can show Helen a little friendliness and say hello.'

'I'm sorry, but . . .'

'She'll be hurt if she thinks you can't be bothered to see her.'

He chose a lie she might accept. 'She's more than sensible enough to understand that work comes before pleasure.'

'That's being silly. What is supposed to be so urgent?'

'Getting things ready for my trip to Oxford.'

'When's that?'

'Tomorrow.'

'You've never mentioned this.' Her tone had a frosty edge to it and the lines deepened around the rim of her eyes.

'Because I only learned about it this morning,' he offered nonchalantly.

'I think you're lying.'

'I'm sorry you believe that's possible.' Ansell feigned an interest in the piece of paper in front of him as her tone grew more aggressive.

'You're going to see her. The woman on the ship.'

The reference to Melanie startled him and he nearly said, with angry bitterness, that this was now very unlikely considering she seemed to have decided not to see him again. 'Eileen, the only time I had any contact with a female on the ship was when there was a dance.'

'And you danced with her.'

'Being charitable, with a couple of middle-aged ladies who lacked partners.'

'She gave you that monkey.'

'Barbary ape.'

'That's right, be pedantic. Babs says you're always trying to be smart.'

'How could she judge?'

'If you go to Oxford to see her, I won't be here when you return.'

'Is that a threat or a promise?'

'You . . . you . . .'

'How about "bastard"?'

She left.

Before the cruise, before he had met Melanie, he had never bothered to argue with Eileen, believing the only reasonable response was silence to deaden her words. Having dined with Aphrodite, he had lost the art of silence and he felt liberated by finally saying what he actually thought to the woman's face.

Belinda drove up the muddy farm track, stopped in front of the farm shed into which a man had just walked. She put on brightly coloured wellington boots, entered an eight standing milking parlour. The man she had seen earlier was cleaning the floor of the pit with hose and squeegee. He moved so he could see her between two milking points. 'I'm not buying.'

'I'm not selling.' With an interest in the countryside, she was not surprised by his sour comment; farmers, betrayed by governments, had to work all hours of the day to make less than the average wage. 'I'm Detective Constable Draper. Have you a minute or two to spare?'

He propped the squeegee against the wall of the pit, twisted the hose muzzle to stop the flow of water, climbed up to ground level. 'Sorry, thought you was from the co-op, trying to sell. I'm Len Fuller.'

'How are things going?'

'Like one expects when they're importing cheap milk from the Continent. Are you here about the woman who lived in that cottage near here?'

'That's right.'

'Was she as cut about as the paper said?'

'Worse.'

'Have you found the bugger what did it?'

'Not yet, which is why I'm having a word with anyone who might be able to help us name him.'

'Ain't much good talking to me.'

'You may know something which can help us.'

After a while, he said, 'Then you'd best come along.'

They went into the end section of the shed in which was a hoist and crusher, bags of barley, and several square bales of hay. Fuller moved a bale for her to sit on, another for himself.

'Did you know Melanie Caine?' she asked.

'Talked to her when I saw her, but that weren't so often.'

'Did she ever say anything about herself? You know, what she did, did she travel a lot, have many friends, all that.'

'Just had a chat. She'd ask how the cows was doing, was they milking well.'

'Was she friendly with someone in the area who'd have known her quite well?'

'There's Mavis, lives next to Cloverdean Cottage. She knows more about others than they knows themself.'

She smiled. 'There's always someone like that in a village. You'll have heard the cottage was broken into and turned upside down?'

'Aye.'

'Is there any talk of who might have done that?'

'No.'

'Must have caused a lot of noise.'

'Likely, but the place is on its own and with woods around three sides, sound wasn't going far.'

Further conversation failed to provide any information of value. Belinda thanked him for his help, reassured him they'd identify the person responsible for murdering Melanie and make certain he was jailed for life.

She drove the half mile to Cloverdean Cottage, a small, rock-built, single-floor house, surrounded on three sides by woodland. Fuller was right, sound would have been muffled. She walked along the road to a clapboard bungalow.

After fifteen minutes, she learned Mavis was eighty-two, the doctor had thought she was going to die when she was born, but he had given her some brandy; she had heard or seen nothing when Cloverdean Cottage had been broken into; what were the police doing, to allow such things to happen. She had spoken to Melanie Caine several times, trying to be friendly, but the other wasn't the friendly kind. That was, she added, not with women.

'She was friendly with men?'

'Must've been,' Mavis replied cryptically.

'Why d'you say that?' Belinda pushed for more information.

'Seen 'em coming and going. Then there's the way she dressed and the jewellery didn't come from nowhere.'

'She might have enjoyed seeing people, especially men, and have had had a private income.'

'If you ask me, she didn't keep herself private.'

It took a woman to judge one. Or perhaps she had picked up the inference in papers and on the TV that Melanie was very promiscuous. Belinda thanked her, drove to the crossroads which marked the centre of the village – four houses, two bungalows, a public house now closed because of lack of trade following the increased penalties for driving when under the influence.

A wasted evening.

Television and the Internet had become both a threat and a boon to criminals. A threat because of CCTV cameras; a boon because one could call up images of every house in the country, saving time and problems when surveying the surrounding area of a potential job. Noyes used the feature on his tablet to bring up Bracken Lane, Frithton and especially number thirty-four. He swore. The garden was much larger than expected and that, plus the recent rain, must make the task of finding where the monkey had been burned many times more difficult.

The Ansell woman would have to tell them where to search.

After a further half hour, during which time there was no movement along Bracken Lane, Tiny – six foot one tall – leaned forward in the car and spoke aggressively. 'You waiting until it's daylight so as we can see better?'

Noyes was reluctant to move just yet, but if tension became too sharp, mistakes would be made. 'OK.'

Jock opened the wrought-iron gate slowly. Tiny followed, an encased electronic reader in his right hand. Lofty used a torch on which the beam had been reduced by plumber's tape to a very small spotlight, scanned the side wall to determine the make of the alarm, evidenced by the shape and size of its cover, binoculars to read the model number. Piera was silent, since it was Noyes' job to make the break in. Noyes gave the signal for them to move.

They went down the passage between house and wooden fencing of the next property and round to the back door. Lofty shone the torch through the kitchen window, fixed the light on the alarm control board. 'Never leave anything to chance' had become his motto after his first arrest. He told Jock to hold the torch and keep it aimed at the board while he used the binoculars to confirm that the layout matched his identification of the model.

He used skeleton keys to force the locks of the door. These had been made by a man whose skill was mostly turned to overhauling and repairing stolen watches and removing identification marks. The skeleton keys had the appearance of twisted wire, but had been made from the highest quality steel and topped to prevent scratch marks – the giveaway that a lock had been forced and also of the skill of the operator.

Lofty went into the kitchen and across to the control panel. Not certain how long it would be before the alarm sounded if the correct numbers weren't fed into the panel in the preprogrammed time, he switched on the electronic reader, held it against the panel. A torrent of figures crossed the small screen and as the seconds passed, they prepared to run. Then figures stilled, leaving one number; within twenty-five seconds there were five more. These were punched in.

They climbed the stairs. The third tread from the top squeaked and caused them to tense, but there was no response. In turn, the others stepped over the noisy tread.

There were four doors leading off the landing. Tiny, using a converted stethoscope, listened at each at some length. He indicated that only one bedroom was occupied. Noyes stood by the door, gripped the handle and turned it slowly, then very gently pushed – the door was not locked. Making certain the others were ready to follow him, he reached inside and felt along the wall to locate the light switch, pressed it down, threw open the door and rushed into the room.

A woman was in the right-hand single bed. In the brief interval between her waking and understanding, Noyes reached the bed before she opened her mouth to scream. 'Shut up or I'll throttle you,' he said violently, as he gripped her throat.

He felt her collapse, become limp. He reached under the nightdress – there was no heart beat.

Jock stared at Eileen. 'She don't look so good.'

'She ain't.'

'She told you where to look?'

'No.'

'Then . . .?'

'The silly bitch has died on us.'

Barbara looked at her watch. Eleven thirty-three. Eileen, who prided herself on never being late, had said she'd be along for coffee at eleven. Pride goes before a fall, Barbara thought, incorrectly but with satisfaction.

She picked up her mobile and dialled. There was no answer. It would be suitable, if annoying, should the invitation have been forgotten. Some weeks ago, she had missed tea at Eileen's where she was to meet someone 'she was bound to like'. Eileen's annoyance had been excessive and frequently regurgitated.

Barbara made coffee for herself. There were chocolate cupcakes, bought in part because Eileen hesitated to eat between meals, but found it difficult to resist temptation and it was amusing to watch the mental battle. Barbara ate a third cupcake, happy in the knowledge that life allowed her to indulge without putting on weight.

Experts said that to eat healthily, one should not have too many ready-cooked meals. When entertaining guests, Barbara always made it clear that all the meals in her house were home-cooked; however, when she and her husband were on their own, finding cooking an unwelcome chore, they repeatedly ate ready-made meals, usually from Marks and Spencer since these were frequently named the best that one could buy.

She was in the supermarket when her name was called out. She turned to see Yvonne, a woman whose husband made so much money, she believed she walked two feet higher off the ground than the plebs.

'I've been trying to get in touch for days and days, but your phone forever seems engaged.'

'I keep telling myself, I must cut back on my social life,' Barbara said with a giggle that was meant to suggest amused exaggeration, but really just underlined that she was trying to prove how popular she really was.

They chatted, much to the annoyance of other shoppers who had to walk around them.

'I must go,' Yvonne finally said. 'We have a German and his wife coming to lunch – he's something to do with Phil's work and I must see Kathy is not making a hash of the meal . . . That's rather fun. A hash!'

Juvenile, Barbara thought.

'It'll be a simple meal. One doesn't want to appear to be trying too hard.'

'Sausages and mash?'

'Just lobster, boeuf-en-croute and chocolate raspberry gateau.'

'Only three courses?'

'Allows one to enjoy the food rather than eating so much the taste buds become overloaded,' Yvonne replied rather pompously.

'I suppose that's sensible. Except . . .'

'What?'

'Germans are usually such good trenchermen. I'd be worried they'd find three courses rather light fare, as an Edwardian would.'

'Different days.'

'Well, I hope all goes smoothly and your Kathy doesn't overcook the beef, as so many do when it's a dish they seldom prepare. Spare a thought for me – lamb and mousse. Very plebeian, but as I always say, none the worse for that . . . You're very friendly with Eileen.'

'I think I would prefer to say just friendly. She can be rather . . . You know . . . Perhaps I should have asked her and David along since she speaks German.'

'Kitchen German. But your guests might find that more homely. By the way, d'you know where she is?'

'No.'

'I can't get through to her on the phone. David's not there, gone up north on work or something. Glad to get out of the way.'

'Why?'

'You've not heard?'

'Not yet.'

'He's been on a cruise and had fun with a blonde.'

'Knowing him, it seems unlikely, but he needs something to cheer him up. I must dash.' Yvonne left.

Barbara went to the food counters to buy lunch.

ELEVEN

Olive Kelton, old enough to have become an uncertain cyclist, wheeled her bicycle across the pavement and down the side alleyway, leaned it against the kitchen wall. She brought an apron and pair of soft shoes out of the handlebar basket, took the key from her purse, walked towards the back door, but was surprised to find it ajar when she went to unlock it. Mrs Ansell was usually very careful about keeping doors shut and locked when at home on her own.

She opened the door, stepped inside. 'Mrs A?' she called out. Silence. After a few seconds of listening out for a delayed answer, she began to worry. Mrs Ansell had said the two of them would take down the curtains in the dining room for dry-cleaning today. 'Mrs A?' she called once more. When there still was no reply, Mrs Kelton recalled the number of burglaries there had been in the neighbourhood recently. Perhaps the open back door meant something more ominous than just a one-off mistake . . .?

She wondered if she should go inside to take a look and try and find out what had happened to the silent Mrs Ansell. However, upon reflection – and there had been all those recent burglaries – she decided instead to call the police. They might laugh at her fears, but that was preferable to being attacked by a teenage thug who was still inside, rummaging around for anything that would help to finance his drug habit.

PC Urquhart stood inside the hall and listened to Olive's convoluted description of what she had seen and not heard.

'Suppose you stay here while I have a good look around, madam. Make some tea,' he added; it might calm her down to be doing something and he wouldn't mind a cup. 'And make sure you don't touch the handles of the back door.'

As he moved into the kitchen and through into the hallway, PC Urquhart became aware of a slight smell which was worrying since it reminded him of the time he had been called to a house in which a man had died.

The old cleaner had told him that she had not searched the downstairs rooms. He did so now and found nothing to indicate vandals or thieves had been there. As he climbed the stairs, the obnoxious smell became more noticeable. With mounting certainty, he entered each room. He was unsurprised when, in the second bedroom, a woman lay dead on the bed, her dishevelled nightdress and bedclothes in disarray around her.

PC Urquhart called in the discovery and then prepared himself for the undoubted histrionics he would have to deal with from the old biddy downstairs, who had hopefully by now made a lovely steaming pot of tea.

The forensic pathologist visually examined the dead woman's eyes. He stood up, crossed to where Glover stood.

'The marks on the neck are too faint to categorize; the post-mortem may be able to say whether the skin has been bruised by pressure or not. However, there are no pinpoint haemorrhages in the eyes as one would expect in a case of throttling.'

'Then for the moment, there's no positive cause of death?' Glover queried.

'That's the picture.'

'Very helpful!' Glover had spoken less lightly than intended.

'We aren't omniscient.'

'Any more than we are.' He wondered whether to add something more to lessen the other's annoyance at what he had said, decided not. 'How about time of death?'

'Around two days ago. Rigor has passed, there's staining on the abdomen.'

'So until the PM we can't be medically certain we're dealing with a crime?'

'No.'

The pathologist left. Glover crossed to the window and looked out at the street, his mind asking the question whether he should treat this as a probable murder before the PM was held. To do so, would tie up many man-hours when he had many other cases to deal with, not least the murder of the presumed high-class hooker, Melanie Caine, which was still causing him much concern. However, should this death prove to have been an unnatural one – particularly a possibility with those very faint marks on the neck – and he hadn't initiated a murder investigation straightaway, this would mean an unwelcome delay as the first twenty-four hours could be all important. One scenario could be that the intruder might have gone into the house to steal, found the owner had died from natural causes, been scared by the danger in which he'd placed himself and fled, taking and disturbing nothing. Such circumstances had occurred. Although, in all likelihood, surely a burglar, finding himself in such a situation, would have taken advantage of it; better be blamed for doing something than doing nothing. So, no, that settled it, her death would be treated as murder as Glover was instinctively convinced there was more to this death than was so far evident.

The rain finally ceased by the middle of the afternoon. In the main bedroom of number thirty-four, curtains had been taken down and carpet rolled up, ready to be taken to the forensic laboratory; window, furniture and inbuilt cupboard had been checked for prints and other traces. The silver-backed hair brushes, small jewellery case in which were three rings, attractive but probably of no great value, and fifty-two pounds, suggested theft had not been an intruder's intention, unless – there was almost always an 'unless' – he had been so shocked to find Mrs Ansell dead, he had fled with nothing.

A search, less concentrated, was in progress in the second bedroom when the phone in the hall rang.

'Answer it,' Glover shouted.

Detective Constable Trent, downstairs, did so. Before he could speak, the female caller said, 'Eileen, where on earth have you been? I've rung a dozen times and no reply. Have you decided that what's good for him is good for you and been having fun while hubby's up north?'

'Who is speaking?' Trent asked.

'Hullo! Hullo! Let me guess what you look like. Six feet, curly black hair, deep blue eyes, pearly white teeth, lips which caress like duck's down.'

'Who is speaking?' he asked for the second time.

'I promise I won't tell, so you don't have to worry.'

'I am Detective Constable Trent.'

'Good God!'

'And you are who?'

'Has someone stolen the family silver?'

'I am very sorry to have to tell you that Mrs Ansell has died.'

'Christ!'

He hoped she was not too shocked. One job that disturbed his cheerful life was to have to report a sudden death and know the listener was probably precipitated into mental darkness. 'Presumably you're a friend of Mrs Ansell, so may I have your name and address, madam?'

'Why d'you want to know them?'

'Someone may need to have a word with you to help us work out what happened.'

'Why.'

'In order to make certain what was the cause of death and to contact her next-of-kin.'

'It must have been heart failure.'

'She was suffering from a problem with her heart?' DC Trent reached inside his jacket pocket to bring out his notebook.

'As fit as a fiddle, but why else would she suddenly die?'

'Your name and address, please?' he insisted again.

She gave them this time, finally overcoming the shock of what she'd heard.

'Are you married?'

'Yes . . .?'

'Is your husband with you?'

'Not at the moment.'

'An officer may soon be along to talk to you.'

He replaced the receiver, went upstairs, spoke to Glover. 'The caller was a woman, sir, who gave her name as Barbara Morley. She did not know Mrs Ansell had died.'

'Had she any particular reason for phoning?'

'She'd tried several times before and got no answer.'

'She's a friend?'

'A close one from the sound of things. She thought I was

Mrs Ansell's boyfriend and we were having fun because her husband was not at home.'

'Having explained the unlikely mistake of that, what did you say?'

'That an officer would probably be along to have a chat with her.'

'What kind of person does she sound like?'

'Bouncy.'

'In ancient language?'

'I'd say she's relatively young and full of fun.'

'In your definition of "fun"? Did she mention where Ansell was, apart from not being there?'

'I didn't like to rush things, sir. Shall I have a word with her now?'

'Find Draper and tell her to go along.'

'As I've already talked to her, wouldn't it be better if I went?' DC Trent said, an annoyed expression on his face.

'She'll probably bounce less when talking to another woman.'

'Do you know where Draper is?'

'You failed to hear me detail her to question the inhabitants of the other houses along Bracken Lane?'

'I meant, where precisely is she now?'

'Unable to foresee the unforeseeable, I can't answer. Perhaps you might think it reasonable to question the occupants of houses in the road.'

He left number thirty-four and walked to the end of the road, turned into the house on his right-hand side.

An elderly man opened the door. 'Yes?'

Trent introduced himself. 'Hello, sir. I'm afraid I have some bad news. Unfortunately—'

He was interrupted. 'There's a police car at number thirty-four.'

'Just what I was about to explain to you, sir. Sadly, Mrs Ansell has died from—'

'Not even half my age!'

'Has Constable Draper already spoken to you?'

'Len was here earlier and told me about the police car. But he didn't know what they was doing. I said, something's happened, mark my words. Likely some young hooligan broke in. Happens all the time and you blokes don't seem to bother . . .'

Trent moved along one house further down the street. The woman who answered his question said a policewoman – not that she looked like one – had talked to her not long ago. As he entered the front garden of the next house – one of the few not turned into a parking space – Belinda came out through the front doorway.

'Thank God I've finally caught up with you,' he said, trying not to show his irritation.

'Content yourself with coincidence, not divine intervention,' Draper replied with a smile.

Trent had projected a relationship with her soon after she joined the CID, even while he had wondered why he was contemplating it. She was reasonably attractive, but no more, and had a sharpish character, that he found made him feel uncomfortable some of the time. He had been surprised when she had quelled his interest and, being unused to failure, had considered the possibility that she was a lesbian. Only gradually, after his rejection, had he understood why he'd been attracted to her in the first place. She enjoyed life as it was presented, not as she would wish it to be. On top of that, she had a quick sense of humour, honoured loyalty, possessed the mettle to accept without rancour or resentment the snide comments from colleagues and return them with interest, and she would condemn or console where another might lack the wish or the mental force to do so.

He brought his thoughts back to the present. 'The guv'nor said to find you. I've been trying to discover where you'd got to.'

'What's the panic?'

'Barbara Morley rang number thirty-four. Thought I was Mrs Ansell's hobby, said she'd been trying to get through on the phone and was I enjoying the same fun and games as her husband had been. The guv'nor wants you to chat to her and find out what's the story. He seems to think you'll likely learn more than I would.'

'Knows you'd have trouble keeping your mind on line,' she said with a knowing smile.

'Some women are complimented by admiration,' Trent replied, trying to sound suitably nonchalant.

'If they can distinguish that from expectation. Where does she live?'

'Number ten, Elmers Road. That's the next one along.' He pointed in the direction of the street.

They parted. Belinda ignored her car and walked up to the T-junction, turned into Elmers Road. Here, houses were more imposing than in Bracken Lane, many suffering from – or gaining from, depending on one's taste – the advantage of architectural embellishments.

The bell ring by the front door was set in an elaborate brass depiction of something, although she couldn't decide what.

Barbara opened the door.

'Mrs Morley?' Belinda asked.

'Yes?'

'I'm Constable Draper.'

'You're here because of poor Eileen . . . So sudden and unexpected, that so charming a person should be taken so early . . .'

No tears, no sobs to underline her over-expressed distress, Belinda noted. 'I should like to have a word with you, if that would be convenient, please.'

'When there's been such shocking news, I feel . . . I feel it is wrong to do anything but grieve.'

Belinda had not often seen fewer signs of grief. 'I'm afraid it's necessary,' she insisted as she edged her way nearer the front door.

'When I know nothing?'

'We have to understand the background to her death and you may well be able to help us.'

'Why?'

'There is the possibility it was not due to natural causes.'

'What are you getting at?'

'She may have been the subject of a fatal assault.'

'Oh, my God!' Barbara stepped back, holding onto the door frame in her distress.

'May I come in?'

'I . . . I suppose so.' She finally backed away and allowed Belinda access through the front doorway and into her house.

The furnishings of the sitting room were expensive and lacked any sense of personality; professional interior decorator, Belinda judged. She sat on a chair which looked as if the designer had been confused, but was surprised to find it comfortable.

'I suppose you'd like a drink' Barbara said.

'No, thank you.'

'I'll have one to try and overcome the terrible news.'

She crossed to an elaborate piece of furniture, pressed a button; bottles and glasses on three shelves came into view. 'You won't change your mind, constable? If you like a malt, I've some Macallan-Glenlivet which is quite pleasant.'

And sufficiently expensive to impress. Belinda repeated her refusal.

'As I said, I really can't think why you have come here.' Barbara sat, a well-filled glass in her hand.

'I hoped that was obvious. I understand you were very friendly with Mrs Ansell?'

'Quite friendly.'

'You'd rung her several times and had no answer which worried you.'

'Naturally.'

'What was your reason to speak to her?'

'There wasn't one. I just felt like having a chat.'

'When your call was answered, you spoke to a policeman, but because he did not have the chance to identify himself, you mistook him for Mrs Ansell's lover.'

'That's nonsense,' she said sharply.

'You suggested her affair with him was a tit-for-tat for Mr Ansell's affair with a woman.'

'I would never make such a comment.'

'Constable Trent has quoted what you said to him.'

'He obviously misunderstood me.' She stood, went over to the 'bar', refilled her glass, returned to sit.

'How do you know Mr Ansell had an affair?'

'Not being his confidante, I don't.'

'Constable Trent has testified that that is what you said.'

'Look, whatever he mistakenly thought I meant, I never tittle-tattle. In any case, it's all in the past and poor, poor Eileen is not with us any more.'

'We have to understand what happened.'

'And I always look to the future, not the past.'

'For once, you'll have to make an exception.'

'When you insist like that, you make me feel you're going to try to arrest me.'

'Only if there's cause. When did you last see Mrs Ansell?'

'I can't remember exactly.'

'Whenever it was, did she seem to be reasonably happy?'

'She wasn't really what I'd call a happy person.'

'Did you notice any change in her in the last few weeks?'

'Well, yes, I did.'

'In what way?'

'She became very bitter.'

'D'you know why?'

'It was that monkey.'

'Monkey?'

'Well, David insisted it was called something else. He told Eileen he'd bought it as a memento of the cruise. She didn't believe him.'

'Why not?'

'Mementoes aren't his scene. He'd left it on his bed when Eileen and I went up to the bedroom. I picked it up and it smelled of scent that certainly wasn't Christian Dior's number something or other . . . Did you know that's the most expensive scent in the world?'

'No.'

'Not interested?'

'No, not really . . .'

'Being a policeman you have to focus your mind on what you people think are much less important matters? Well, anyway, Eileen would never have worn anything so mass market as the scent coming off that monkey. Then there were some blonde hairs on the monkey which couldn't have been hers.'

'Why not?'

'A different shade of peroxide.'

'So what did you think this added up to?'

'What any intelligent woman would. He'd been having a few free ones and the girlfriend had hugged the monkey as well as him.'

'Did Mrs Ansell come to the same conclusion?'

'Reckoned he'd been having fun on the cruise and was angry.'

'Cruise?' Belinda repeated sharply.

'Yes.'

'Was he on his own?'

'Not all the time, obviously. If you mean was Eileen there, the company wouldn't pay for her as well as for him.'

'Why were they paying for him?' Belinda sensed she might finally be about to hear some significant information.

'They'd been told to prepare a fresh advertising campaign for the shipping company.'

'What ship was he on?'

'Can't remember.'

'The *Helios*?'

'How d'you guess?'

'Where did the cruise go?'

'It was only a cheapie: the Mediterranean.'

'Did Mrs Ansell ever suspect her husband was having an affair before then?'

'She'd have had to be stupid not to wonder.'

'Why d'you say that?'

'She kept the oats locked up. He was bound to jump at the first opportunity.'

'Their relationship was strained?'

'Almost broken.'

'I imagine you've a reason for thinking that'

'Sometime back I was telling her I'd heard a certain gentleman's idea of pleasure was to . . . Doesn't matter what. And when I chanced to mention that to her, she got all of a twitter and remarked that sex was so demeaning. Of course, I'd guessed how she thought about it when she decided they'd sleep in separate beds. Wouldn't have been long before it turned into different bedrooms.'

'Did she accuse her husband of having had an affair?'

'Yes.'

'How did he respond?'

'Denied it, of course. Have you ever met a husband with the courage to tell his wife he's been rodding around.'

'It happens.'

'I suppose that shouldn't surprise me.'

Belinda's response to the inference that she was gullible was weak and, because of her work, wrong. 'But then I have so little contact with adulterous husbands.'

TWELVE

Belinda walked into the CID general room, spoke to DC Pascall who was writing up some reports on his computer. 'D'you know if the guv'nor's in?'

'Do I not!'

'Is he beginning to ignite?'

'In flames. It took me longer to do some work than he reckoned it should and he all but consigned me to the beat.'

'What's cropped up?'

'The PM on Mrs Ansell can't be carried out yet and we can't get hold of the husband.'

'Then I suppose I'd better don asbestos before reporting.'

'Everything else is delayed, so wait until he's cooled.'

'And give him the chance to fire up again?'

She went along to the DI's room. The door was ajar so she walked in. 'Just back, guv.'

'About time.'

'It's been a bit of a job getting Barbara Morley to talk in-between drinks.'

'Well?'

'Mr Ansell has been on a cruise.'

'So?'

'Aboard the *Helios*.'

Glover showed no surprise. Was she supposed to think that he already knew that? She continued, 'On-board, he met a woman whom Barbara reckons kept him from being lonely at night.'

Glover fidgeted with a pencil. 'If Melanie Caine was in the diamond racket and Ansell was the man aboard who looked at her as if he'd just discovered sex . . . Phone the hotel and find out if Ansell has turned up yet.'

'They promised to get in touch with us the moment he did.'

'Would it disturb you to do as I ask right now?'

Belinda took her cue and left his office. Ten minutes later, she gained slight satisfaction in reporting that Ansell had not returned to the hotel and the staff would have been in touch with her, as requested, had he done so.

As DC Trent had learned, life often kicked one in the nuts. Because he was on night duty, Alan – until now a so-called friend – had seized the chance to ask Christine out for a meal. What on earth had induced her to accept an invitation from a man who preferred cider to real ale, enjoyed poetry, visited art galleries and wasn't afraid to admit he liked studying birds? He'd asked Christine how could any man waste time watching birds. 'Isn't that your favourite occupation?' she'd replied tartly.

Trent's bleak thoughts were interrupted by the phone.

'Park Hotel. You've twice asked us to inform you when Mr Ansell returned. He has just done so.'

Trent rang Glover's home.

His wife answered.'Yes?'

'Constable Trent, Mrs Glover.'

'What d'you want?'

Like the wives of officers of senior rank in the armed forces, she assumed their curt authority. 'May I speak to the inspector, please?'

'Is that necessary?'

Of course, he was only ringing for the fun of it. 'I'm afraid so.'

'He is very tired, so be as brief as possible.'

He hoped Christine would demand to be driven home straight after the meal and not accept a suggestion that they drove down to the coast and watched the lights of passing ships as Alan demonstrated superior intellect by babbling about rusty British coasters with salty funnels.

'Yes?' Glover said as a challenge, not a greeting.

'I've been phoned by Park Hotel, sir. Mr Ansell has just returned there.'

'Anything else to report?'

'No, guv.'

'Keep it that way.'

PC Brownley walked up to the reception desk at Park Hotel, explained he wanted to give Mr Ansell a message to prevent the clerk's imagination moving into overdrive. 'Wanted to give' was the ultimate hypocrisy, he thought bitterly.

Moments later, Ansell walked out of the lift, crossed to the reception desk, was directed to where Brownley was waiting. He came to a stop. 'You want a word? What about?'

'Perhaps we might go up to your room, sir, and I'll explain.'

'Why can't you tell me now?'

'I would prefer to speak to you when we were on our own, sir.'

Ansell's mind ranged over the possibilities which could cause a PC to come to the hotel, failed to approach the truth. 'Very well.'

The lift took them up to the fourth floor, an electronic card gave access to the room.

'What's the problem?' Ansell asked sharply.

Brownley spoke nervously, certain that the memory of Ansell's shock and grief would haunt him for days, cause him to look at his wife and perversely visualize the pain of learning she was dead. 'I am sorry, Mr Ansell, I have to give you some tragic news.'

'Yes, I know. What's happened to her?' he asked harshly, concerned because of Melanie's telephone call, the frantic demand he return Georgie immediately, the horror in her voice when he had said the monkey was burned, and then the way in which the call had been abruptly terminated. He had recently been living with the certainty that she had been in grave danger.

'What's happened to her?' he asked harshly, convinced of the identity of whom they were speaking.

'I am very much afraid your wife has died, sir.'

'My wife?' Ansell repeated, his confusion obvious.

'You do understand what I have just said, Mr Ansell?' PC Brownley, his own confusion considerable, felt he needed to reiterate the gravity of the situation.

'Yes.'

'You will understand you should return home as soon as possible.'

Ansell again said nothing.

Brownley's confusion became suspicion.

* * *

The pathologist finished dictating into a recorder, asked the SOCOs if there were any further examinations they required; there was none. He turned away from the table on which Eileen Ansell's body lay, indicated to the mortuary assistant to reconstruct it so it could be viewed by the husband or relative to confirm identity.

He spoke to Glover. 'Can't offer you much, Jim.' The use of Christian names between pathologist and senior detective had become quite common. 'There are no signs of trauma, asphyxiation, or indication of disease. With regard to the marks on the neck which were noted, these have become virtually imperceptible. The tissues below provided inconclusive evidence. In my opinion, fingers may have been applied to the neck, but only briefly and without much force.'

'She wasn't throttled?'

'No.'

'Then what did she die from?'

'The negatives offer the possibility of overwhelming fear that she was about to be throttled and she suffered from vagal inhibition. A victim in fear of personal injury may suddenly die; there are several reports of a prostitute gripped by the neck, going out in a flash.'

'Can you say that that's what was the cause of death?'

'No.'

'Then your report is going to state what?'

'That because of the facts, I can only surmise, not give a firm conclusion.' The pathologist shrugged his shoulders as he gave what he knew was an unwelcome decision for Glover – indeed for any investigating officer of an unexplained death.

Glover hurried from his car, into divisional HQ, and up to his office. Through no fault of his, he was late. Strict time-keeping by all was one of his demands. As he sat at his desk, Frick entered.

'Morning, sir. PC Brownley has been trying to ring you from Oxford.'

'Trying to ring you' made it obvious his delay had been noted. Frick had a solid nature, accepting criticism without notable resentment or praise with clear pride, yet occasionally he slyly made his thoughts evident.

'I suggested you phoned him back, sir, so that he made his report directly to you. The number is on your desk.'

'You did not find out if his report was going to be of any use?'

'He seemed to think it was rather important, but did sound slightly confused.'

'And you're leaving me to sort out his confusion. Have you drawn up today's calendar?'

'On the desk.'

'Any movement in naming who's been flashing around the green in Esley Common?'

'Not so far. It's like my first inspector used to say, one can't make bricks without clay.'

'The Romans made concrete from volcanic ash.'

'Very ingenious people.'

As Frick left, Glover picked up the receiver of the outside phone, dialled the number he had been given. He asked to speak to Constable Brownley.

'Inspector Arnold here, inspector. Brownley is off duty, but has left me with his report. If you'll give me your number, I'll fax it to you.'

He thanked the other, replaced the phone, studied the list of current and pending cases and the officers expected to be called to court. More men away from direct duty.

He was brought the fax. He read it once, then again. He stared through the window. Brownley had been surprised by Ansell's manner. He had not been nearly as shocked as was to be expected. No tears, no mind-shattered cry to be told it wasn't true. 'Yes, I know'. Had he steeled his emotions because a friend had already informed him his wife had died? Yet how could such a friend have had the opportunity to do so before Ansell left the hotel in the morning and from which he had been absent until now? Brownley named him bewildered, but not showing the signs of bitter grief which one would expect. It was hardly surprising Brownley had seemed confused. He lacked the knowledge of the background to the case and could only judge by experience.

Glover let his imagination roam. The phone rang. Glover ignored it as he recalled Barbara Morley's muddled phone conversation from which Belinda had gained reason to believe Ansell had enjoyed an affair on the *Helios*. Hellan, the bar steward, had mentioned a man who, when drinking at the bar with Melanie, was mentally rogering her. Asked to describe the man, Hellan had failed to do so to any effect. But if her partner had been Ansell, he might have assumed Brownley's warning of tragic news could briefly have made him think the subject was Melanie . . .

The phone rang. He once again ignored it.

Ansell's home in Bracken Lane had been secured since the finding of his wife's body. It would be unusual if there were not a photograph of him somewhere about the house. That photograph could easily be transmitted to the *Helios* . . .

The phone rang. He swore as he lifted the receiver.

'So a cat may speak to a king!' Anne said. 'It's taken me half a dozen attempts to get through to you.'

'Two.'

'You sound sharp so I'll be brief. Will you promise to go out to dinner on Saturday, whatever happens?'

'No.'

'There are times when I wonder why I married you.'

'You know fixing a definite time can get blown to hell. Who's been unwise enough to try to make me name one?'

'The Wilkins. And since in your present mood you'll tell me you don't know who they are, Eric's parents.'

'Why do they want to dine and wine us?'

'Because they haven't met you more than a couple of times. Is work being extra stressful?'

'Yes.'

'Then come back at a reasonable time, I'll cook you a good meal, you'll provide a nice wine, and you'll relax.'

'Forget it.'

'Duck paté, roast beef, Yorkshire puds, chocolate almond pudding.'

'I only want cheese and salad.'

'Lighten up, darling.'

'How many times have I said . . .'

'I've never been able to count that high. We want to be on good terms with the Wilkins and if you make it seem as if you're reluctant to meet them, it could make all sorts of problems for Shirley and Eric. Incidentally, they're trying to fix a wedding day.'

'When she's only eighteen . . .'

'Stop being possessive.'

'How's he going to keep her?'

'By working.'

'In his job, as yet he can't be paid much.'

'She'll keep working.'

'Until she's pregnant.'

'You're becoming quite impossible. Don't forget, if money becomes very tight for them, they can start fiddling social security . . . Do I need to explain that's meant to be funny? When you're more approachable than a grizzly bear with toothache, we can discuss things.' She rang off.

If she had to deal with as many cases as the CID concerning the bitter, often violent rows between couples who had married too young for their characters and lack of maturity . . . He called himself several choice names for allowing the black side of his job to threaten the white side of his life. After all, Eric seemed to be relatively intelligent and was surprisingly respectful for the present generation . . .

Belinda entered. 'You want something, sir?'

He picked up a photograph which had been in number thirty-four. 'Show this to Fred Hellan on the *Helios*. Find out if he can identify this man as the one he knew as Taffy, who drank with Melanie Caine and looked at her as if . . . Never mind what. As quick as you like.'

She picked up the photograph. 'I'll fax or email this later . . .'

'You fail to understand my order?'

'Which is difficult, though not impossible.'

'What the devil does that mean?'

'A day or two back, I got in touch with the Rex Cruising Company to find out how long the *Helios* would be in harbour. I thought we needed to know, should we wish to get in touch with anyone aboard.'

'Good thinking.'

His praise was appreciated.

'What did you learn?'

'It sailed a couple of days ago on another Mediterranean cruise.'

'Then follow your suggestion. Send the request to the captain in official terms and in the name of the detective chief superintendent to add weight since the captain may be over-conscious of his rank.'

'A common failing.'

'Do you have Australian blood in you?'

'Why d'you ask?'

'You have a habit of denigrating authority.'

She smiled, left.

THIRTEEN

The email from MV *Helios* was received just after ten on a morning of grey cloud, intermittent drizzle, and a shifting wind; a day on which not to imagine those on the *Helios* enjoying cloudless skies.

Belinda took the printed message to Glover's room. 'Just come though from the *Helios*, guv.'

'Does it answer the question?'

She passed the paper across.

He read, swore, did not apologize as normally he would have done in defiance of canteen culture. 'Why the devil was a useless photo sent?'

'It wasn't.'

'You fail to understand what this says?' Glover shook the papers at her to reiterate his annoyance.

'You chose which photo to send so I'm sure it was the sharpest.'

'Then they mucked things up in communication. Tell them to make certain it gets through clearly this time.'

She went over to the door.

'By the way, I came across an old book of nursery rhymes, printed before anyone had heard of political correctness. You remember my asking what Taffy did?'

'No.'

'"I went to Taffy's house, Taffy was not at home, Taffy came to my house and stole a marrowbone".'

She left.

Not long afterwards she was called back to Glover's room. 'Are you ready?' he asked.

'For what?'

'As I said, to go and question Ansell.'

She was about to remind him he had not expressed that intention but for once decided to remain silent.

They went down to the car park.

'Shall I drive, sir?' Normally he preferred her to do so since it gave him time to brood.

'I will,' he said and accelerated off before she'd barely shut the car door and settled into her seat.

As they turned into Bracken Lane, he said, 'I'll do all the talking; is that clear?'

'Of course,' she agreed. A snarky superior was a fact of life, but it was unusual for the DI to growl so often.

There was room to park directly in front of number thirty-four. He did not immediately turn off the engine but stared through the side window. 'With the rates as high as they are, you need a bob or two to live here.'

'To live anywhere.'

The PC by the front door looked as bored as he felt; the monotony of standing guard at a crime scene was one of the more disliked tasks. 'Morning, sir. Mr Ansell is inside.'

Glover walked up to the front door, pressed the bell. The door was opened by Olive Kelton, the cleaner. 'Yes?' she asked suspiciously, taking her job as gatekeeper very seriously.

'We're here to speak to Mr Ansell.'

'He ain't seeing anyone.'

'I'm afraid he has to see us, Mrs Kelton.'

'How d'you know my name?'

'I'm Inspector Glover, my companion is Constable Draper.'

She spoke more aggressively. 'Then it must be a good time for the yobbos with all you lot here.'

'We've called out the reserves to spoil their fun.'

She was briefly uncertain whether he was serious or making fun of her. 'I suppose you'd best come in, but don't worry him rotten like the others did.'

They went into the hall. As Inspector Glover was clearly not going to speak, Belinda thought it might be more fruitful to be polite and try to get the redoubtable Mrs Kelton on side. 'We are sorry to have to be here and will be away as soon as possible, you can be assured of that, Mrs Kelton.'

Olive's annoyance ebbed slightly. 'He's real bust up.'

'Of course he is and we fully understand.'

'Then . . .' She pointed. 'He's in there.'

They went into the sitting room. Ansell, slumped in a chair, saw Belinda and came to his feet.

'Good morning, Mr Ansell,' Glover said.

He did not return the greeting.

'I'm Inspector Glover and my companion is Constable Draper. We'd like to have a word or two with you.'

Ansell said nothing.

'Do you mind if we sit?'

'Of course not.'

Once seated, Glover said, 'We're here to ask a few questions which—'

Draper interrupted her boss. Official behaviour was all very well until one faced a man who looked as if he'd lost everything, including hope. 'We apologize for bothering you at so sad a time, Mr Ansell, and would not think of doing so were it not necessary.'

'Quite.' Glover contained his annoyance at her interruption to the single word. 'Mr Ansell, I have to inform you that Mrs Ansell suffered from no disease or damage to internal organs. However, when first medically examined, individual marks on her neck were noted. They later almost disappeared and there was no indication of internal bruising, yet there is the possibility that fingers were placed on her neck.'

'What are you saying?'

'Had there been lasting external and internal bruising, there would have been evidence as to the cause of death.'

'I don't understand.'

'There are circumstances in which a person's body closes down and there seems to be no physical reason for its doing so. This is called vagal inhibition and is caused by violent shock or extreme fear. It seems possible that such was the cause of Mrs Ansell's death, but medically one cannot be certain. Consequently, we have to learn whether there were circumstances which make it likely that she had reason to suffer overwhelming shock or fear.'

'Then someone must have broken into the house,' Ansell muttered.

'Naturally, we are considering that.'

As Glover knew, the locks of the outside doors of the house had been examined with the aid of an illuminated lock probe and there had been no sign of the scratches to be expected had they been forced with the aid of skeleton keys. Glover continued, 'Are there many valuable articles in this house – jewellery, paintings, antique furniture or pottery, that sort of thing?'

'No valuable antiques, not much jewellery. Eileen . . . My wife had the usual sort of things – rings, bracelet, necklace which she frequently wore, but all the jewellery she inherited from an aunt is kept at the bank.'

'Then why would someone believe it worth breaking into here?'

'I've no idea.'

'Then probably the person was what we call, an opportunist. The security system was not switched on. Were you not in the habit of having it on at night?'

'She must have forgotten.'

'It wasn't part of the normal routine of closing down the house before going to bed?'

'Yes. I always did that, but I was in Oxford.'

'It didn't occur to you to mention the alarms when you phoned her that night?'

'I didn't phone. When I had to be away because of work, I seldom did unless there was a specific reason.'

'One could say it had become a settled marriage,' Glover said lightly. Would any wife forget to set the alarms when on her own? he wondered. Would not most wives expect to hear from their husbands when they were away? 'I understand you are friendly with Mrs Morley.'

'My wife . . . was.'

'You would not call her a friend?'

'I find her too interested in other people's lives.'

'Then you perhaps will not be surprised to learn she believes you had an affair when aboard the *Helios*?'

The indirect question shocked Ansell.

'Did you become over-friendly with someone on the cruise?'

'No.'

'There's no truth in her suggestion?'

'It's one of her bloody lies.'

The door opened and Olive entered the room. 'That's enough!'

'What the devil d'you think you're doing?' Glover demanded.

'You ain't the Gestapo, so clear off.'

'I've a damned good mind . . .' Glover began but was once again interrupted by his subordinate.

'You're right, Mrs Kelton, we've been here rather a long time. We'll go and leave Mr Ansell in some peace.' Belinda stood.

Glover's expression showed thoughts he did not immediately put into words. He remained silent as he said goodbye, led the way out of the house and only spoke when they were in the car. 'What the hell did you think you were up to?' he demanded harshly.

'Couldn't you understand the emotional torment he's suffering? How would you cope if you were at the bottom of the world and someone uninvited turned up and bullied you?'

'D'you think you're running this case?'

She started the engine and drove off. There was silence until they were stopped by lights.

'When I was a DC, I very quickly learned to keep my mouth shut when the DI was questioning someone,' Glover said.

The lights changed, she engaged first gear and drew away.

FOURTEEN

The email arrived at 10.15 the next morning. Belinda, who had been scanning her email in box impatiently ever since she'd sat down at her desk that morning, was relieved to have an answer at last. Hellan had identified the second photograph as that of the man who had been very friendly with Melanie Caine.

She went up to the DI's office; the door was half open, so she walked in. 'Just arrived, guv.' She handed Glover the printed-out sheet of paper.

He read the message. 'Then we need another word with Ansell. And that woman who works there will get on with her job and not interfere.'

'Her determination to protect him from hassle says a lot for him as an employer, I suppose,' Draper pointed out.

'More likely that no one will now be checking the plates are clean.'

'You're very short on sentiment today.'

'Have you any more personal remarks to make before you do as asked?'

'You want me to get the car to the front door?'

'To tell Sergeant Frick to go with me so I can conduct an interview uninterrupted and at the pace I choose.'

He watched her leave. She reminded him how, at home, Anne never withheld an opinion or a criticism she considered, often mistakenly, valid. His thoughts moved sequentially. Was Shirley sufficiently mature to marry; how would she cope with the problems which so often followed the honeymoon?

Frick entered, stopped in front of the desk. 'Constable Draper said you wanted to see me, sir.'

'We've received solid confirmation Ansell was very friendly with Melanie Caine on the *Helios*. We'll drive to his place now and have another word with him.'

'I'm tied up in another case at the moment, sir.'

'Untie yourself.'

'Because of it, I'm having to meet the DI from A division.'

'Then tell Trent to come along.'

'He's away.'

'Is anyone around?'

'Constable Draper.'

'Man proposes, the dragon disposes.'

'How's that, sir?'

'The Welsh dragon.'

'Isn't it the leek they go for?'

'Her unwelcome habits seem to be catching. Remind her I am running the case, I do not appreciate her interrupting me and her opinions are only of interest when I ask for them.'

Frick left, a look of humour on his face as if he couldn't wait to impart their DI's latest remarks.

Glover read through a report which was to be sent to county HQ, noted two misspellings, marked them and wrote 'redo'. Publishers of dictionaries must make very little profit from the younger generation. He knew he should probably just write these reports himself, but he did have to admit that he wasn't the most accurate of typists. He supposed he'd have to send himself on some sort of course in the near future.

Belinda entered.

He looked up. 'Sergeant Frick told you what's on?'

'I am to accompany you to question Mr Ansell again, to remember I am not the senior investigating officer, to say nothing unless asked to speak, to ignore the mental pain your questioning will cause Mr Ansell.'

'You can add, to refrain from insolence.'

Moments later she started the engine and backed, turned, waited for a van to pass before she drew out into the road. Their journey to Bracken Lane was quick and silent.

Mrs Kelton, working extra time to help Mr Ansell, as she immediately informed them after opening the door of number thirty-four, opened with: 'Ain't you nothing better to do than keep bothering him?'

'We need to have another talk with Mr Ansell,' Glover stated.

'When you was here barely yesterday? Forgot what you wanted to say, like as not. I'll find out if he wants to see you.'

'He has no—'

Belinda quickly interrupted. 'Once again, we're very sorry, Mrs Kelton, but we'll be as brief as we possibly can be and do our best not to distress him.'

'I suppose you'd best come in.'

Mrs Kelton waited until they were inside and in the sitting room before she said, 'He'll be down when he wants to be.' She closed the door with a bang.

'I suppose I should apologize,' Belinda said sweetly, 'but it seemed better to lighten resentment than increase it.'

Glover glowered at her but had no time to say anything as Ansell entered the sitting room and wished them an unwelcoming good morning. They sat.

'Mr Ansell, you will have understood from what has been said before, we are trying to ascertain whether anyone might have caused Mrs Ansell so great a fright that she suffered from vagal inhibition. On my last visit, I asked if you had met Melanie Caine aboard the *Helios*. You denied this. Do you wish to stand by your denial?'

'Of course.'

'You will understand that if we have cause to believe you did meet her and had an affair with her, we will question why you lied.'

'I did not meet her.'

'A bar steward, Hellan, on the *Helios* has been shown photographs of her and you. He identified you and her as the couple who were frequently together at the bar he served and, in his opinion, you were enamoured with her.'

Ansell tried to quell the panic the statement occasioned. 'He is totally mistaken.'

'The captain of the *Helios* made him give his evidence after swearing to tell the truth on a Bible. An unusual occurrence in unusual circumstances, but one that would probably be accepted in court without objection.'

'He must have reckoned I was a poor tipper.'

'A far-fetched possibility. Mrs Morley believes you had an affair on the ship.'

'She'll think up six impossible slanders before breakfast.'

'She is unlikely to have conceived the affair without reason.'

'Georgie.'

'Would you please explain?'

'I'd met a passenger a few times and we became friendly – in the simple meaning of the word.'

'Was she unmarried?'

'Yes.'

'Her name?'

Ansell gave the first which occurred to him. 'Nancy.'

'And her surname?'

'I don't remember.'

'Your memory was on hold? No doubt we will be able to judge what was her name from the passenger list. Please continue.'

'She bought the Barbary ape in Gibraltar, found she didn't have enough room to pack it in her luggage, asked me if I would take it in mine.'

'Did you?'

'Yes.'

'It did not occur to you that it might be an injudicious thing to do?'

'Why should it have done?'

'You would have known luggage has to pass through customs and anything bought abroad has to be declared. I don't doubt you have read or heard of a passenger who was carrying something illegal who asked someone else to carry it for him through the customs' inspection.'

'She wasn't someone to put anyone else at risk.'

'Was your luggage searched?'

'No.'

'Were you strip-searched?'

'No.'

'Melanie Caine was. What does that suggest to you?'

'She was chosen by chance, as regularly happens.'

'Customs had been advised she would be carrying illegal goods. That she was found without them means she passed them on to someone else.'

'Or that the advice was nonsense.'

'Did you meet this Nancy after you were through customs?

'No.'

'She has been in touch with you since then?'

'No.'

'Then you still have the ape?'

'It was burnt.'

'By you?'

'By my wife.'

'Why did she do that?'

'Because Babs made out that the ape proved I'd had an affair.'

'Describe the ape.'

'A typical tourist memento. The apes at Gibraltar are very carefully looked after because—'

'You may assume we know the tradition. What was it made of?'

'Material with a thick nap.'

'Was it filled with foam?'

'I imagine so.'

'You did not open it up?'

'Why would I do that?'

'You are a man of intelligence and it's reasonable to accept that in the circumstances it must have occurred to you that something was hidden in the ape since this Nancy was scared to take it through customs.'

'Christ! I say the same thing time and again, but you won't listen. I was doing a good deed, not smuggling.'

'I do not believe Nancy existed. The ape was Melanie Caine's and she persuaded you to carry it ashore in your luggage because there were illegally mined, uncut diamonds in it and she suspected, or was certain, she had been eyeballed. So she needed to find someone who would carry them ashore for her. He would have to be easily attracted so the odds were he needed to be a little short of middle-aged, married to a less than amorous wife, on his own and ready to jump at a chance of unbridled sex at which she was an expert.'

Ansell struggled to avoid the humiliation any acceptance of what had just been said must bring him; a humiliation increased still further by the presence of Belinda.

'She was, of course, an upmarket call-girl. And she is

now dead, Mr Ansell. Did you know that?' Glover came out with the bald statement and watched Ansell's reaction closely.

'You know nothing about her . . . What do you mean dead?' He was clearly shocked by that, but couldn't bear the thought of giving himself away.

'But you do or you would not be so disturbed by my description of her. Despite your many denials, Mr Ansell, I am convinced that you met Melanie Caine aboard the *Helios* and had an affair with her.

'The bar steward will not be the only crew member to have noticed the two of you together. A stewardess may well have gained a good insight into the nature of your relationship. The dining staff will bear witness. Are you going to force us to question all these people?'

There was a long silence during which Ansell tried and failed to find a credible way in which to continue his denial. His mind remained numb from the certainty that his worst fears had been realised and that Melanie was actually dead.

Glover accepted the failure as an admission. 'Did Melanie Caine ever suggest what was inside the ape?'

'No.' Ansell muttered in so low a voice, he was asked to repeat what he had said.

'Well, let me tell you,' Glover stated in his matter-of-fact way, 'there were several large uncut diamonds in there. Because she was certain she was being watched by the police, she determined to find someone to bring them in for her.'

Ansell again recalled the frantic way in which Melanie had begged him to return Georgie immediately, her terror when he had said the ape had been burned.

'You said your wife burned the ape. Where did she do that?'

'She wouldn't say, but it had to be in the garden or it would have attracted too much attention.'

'And because of the rain, all signs of the bonfire would have been washed away and you were left with almost no chance of finding the diamonds unless your wife named the precise spot . . . I don't think we need continue for the moment.' He stood, left the sitting room, held the door open for Belinda.

Mrs Kelton came out of the kitchen. 'You finished?'

'Yes.'

'Then clear off and don't come again.'

As he followed Belinda out, he murmured, 'We'll be back, soon.'

Belinda drove the car away from the pavement and down the road, stopped at the T-junction.

Glover said. 'We've made some progress, but it's just managed to raise even more questions.'

She said nothing.

'Ansell was probably responsible for her death and it'll be a smooth mouthpiece who gets a verdict of manslaughter rather than murder.'

She said, 'You're assuming that he was so overwrought when he knew what would happen to Melanie if he didn't return the ape, that he threatened his wife and scared her to death if she didn't tell him where she'd burned it.'

'Yes.'

'He did not admit he was with Melanie.'

'His silence did. And what about his physical reaction when we told him she was dead. He almost collapsed on the spot. And we have a perfect eyewitness. Would you choose to ignore the bar steward's evidence?'

'Photos don't always make for a solid identification.'

'Here, they do. Melanie suspected, or knew, she was under surveillance so she picked him out and dumbed his brain with sex. A not uncommon occurrence, you'll agree.'

'You believe I'm qualified to give an opinion?'

'Goddamn it, all I was saying . . . Small wonder Sergeant Frick once told me that you could be more difficult to deal with than running on water.'

She stopped at lights.

'Melanie induced Ansell to buy her the ape in Gibraltar. She unpicked the stitching, pushed the seven diamonds inside the stuffing, sewed it up. Brain suspended, he cheerfully carried it through customs. Then what?'

She was silent.

'You've become unwilling to give an opinion?' Glover pressed.

'It seems to disturb you when I do,' Draper retorted with her characteristic defiance.

'Well, let me give you my theory,' Glover began. 'Ansell arrived home, stupidly left the ape on the bed where the Morley woman picked it up, smelled cheap scent, saw blonde hairs that hadn't come from her, and declared adultery. Later, Melanie phoned Ansell to tell him where he must meet her and hand over the ape. His wife said she'd burned it. He demanded to know where exactly and threatened her so violently, she was frightened to death.

'That Melanie was tortured must surely mean that whoever was with her when she phoned believed she was trying to double-cross them and skip with the diamonds. Not being an expert, the torturer went too far and she died. Her body was dumped in the woods.

'They must have found the number she dialled and from that were able to identify Ansell's house in Bracken Lane. They broke into it with the help of a very smart twirler, found the wife was on her own, explained what would happen to her if she didn't tell them exactly where she'd burned the ape. She collapsed. To search the large, sodden garden at night was hopeless.

'So the diamonds, which would not have been burned up in any bonfire, are somewhere in the garden. But where?'

She drove into the station car-park and the bay reserved to the DI.

'And answer came there none.'

She opened the door, stepped out of the car. He did the same, spoke to her over the roof. 'When assumptions are linked to facts to provide answers, there is always the chance of a mistaken assumption or fact. Can you name one?'

'No.'

'So far, we've assumed Melanie never hinted or spoke about the diamonds to Ansell and he carried them ashore in naive innocence. But is that a mistake? Could he have become reasonably mentally alert and guessed at least part of what was going on and reckoned to join in. Desperate, for his own sake, not Melanie's, to make his wife say exactly where the bonfire had been, did he inadvertently kill her? Where do we go from here?'

'I'm sure you'll tell me.'

'We see where the diamonds are in the garden.'

'You mean to search it?'

'To have it searched.'

FIFTEEN

The day was fine and warm, but the earth in the garden of number thirty-four remained glutinous, causing the police who were searching it to swear freely.

They found many objects which they named pebbles. But in order to leave no possibility untested, and because he was unsure what they might look like, Glover called in a diamond expert and asked him to say if any of the pebbles might in fact be uncut diamonds. The expert tried not to show his amusement at the suggestion.

The search proved unfruitful in the discovery of anything of the sparkling variety, so Glover reluctantly returned to the station.

Back at his desk, Glover stared at the form lit up on his PC screen which asked for projected costs for the next month. As if any mere copper could provide something so prone to chance and criminals. The force needed soothsayers not accountants. The phone rang.

The caller was Wicks, a DI at county HQ. 'How's it going your way?'

'Slowly.'

'Then you'll be sorry to know the chief will be with you in an hour.'

'It's Friday the thirteenth?'

Wicks laughed.

The call over, Glover picked up a ballpoint and began to write down the questions Abbotts was likely to ask. Again, the phone interrupted him.

'Belinda here, sir.'

She should identify herself as Constable Draper, he thought bad-temperedly. 'What is it now?'

'I've heard from the phone people. Melanie Caine made a call to Ansell just before midnight on Saturday, the eighteenth of last month.'

'Where was the call from?'

'An unidentifiable mobile.'

He replaced the receiver, annoyed he had probably allowed his ill humour to become obvious.

When in his early twenties, Detective Chief Superintendent Abbotts had played rugger with the county police team. A heavily built forward with the ability to run quickly, along with the possession of an aggressive nature, made him a key forward player in a team which won the force's championship three years in a row. As youth slipped away, he had had to give up the energetic and injury-prone sport. Always enjoying food, the lack of exercise had caused bulk to build. This was the imposing figure that entered Glover's office later that morning.

There was a creak as he sat on the desk in Glover's room. 'What's your appreciation?'

Glover repeated much of what he had previously said to Belinda, though in a neutral manner.

'Do you think Mrs Ansell, when on her own at night, might have forgotten to turn on the alarm system?' Abbotts asked.

'Unlikely for that type of woman, I think, unless she had had a skinful and that was negated by the PM.'

'Was she normally a heavy drinker?'

'We have no evidence one way or the other apart from a healthy liver which would imply a moderate intake.'

'Let's accept she did not forget to switch it on, then.'

'Then I'd say among the intruders there had to be an electronics expert and a top twirler. If the numbers needed to still an alarm of that make and model are not noted and have been forgotten by some gormless individual – apparently this does happen – they can be regained, but only with a very smart bit of kit. The outside door locks were checked and none of them showed signs of having been forced. If there was a twirler who managed the job, he could have the Bank of England worried.'

'You think there was a break-in?'

'Not a forced entry.'

'The husband?'

'He's in the frame, even if we can't yet prove he wasn't in Oxford throughout the relevant times.'

'What was the state of the marriage?'

'Almost certainly strained. But there's no evidence of violence. Even the Morley woman, who'd find reason to malign a saint, has not suggested he ever hit his wife. Constable Draper reckons he's incapable of deliberately harming or threatening a woman.'

'Her reason?'

'Womanly intuition.'

'Not much safer than reading a horoscope. Have you checked with records for the names of villains with the skill to break a sophisticated alarm system?'

Glover nodded. 'There are only two names now in the frame and one's been inside for the past two years.'

'The other?'

'Gabby Ayling from up north, occasionally brought down south for a sharp job.'

Abbotts eased himself off the corner of Glover's desk. 'Keep looking and speed things up.'

Glover was irritated by the order.

'Has the wife's body been released for burial?' Abbotts turned back from the door as if the question had just occurred to him, although it was always his tactic to leave a final order for just before he left a room.

'Not yet.'

'Find out the form of burial and have someone at the service to note Ansell's reactions.'

He finally left and Glover got back to imparting his own orders further down the line.

PC Thorn stood in front of the sweets stand in the supermarket and stared at the boxes of truffles. Could any man understand women? The previous night, Carol might have been in an icebox.

'Evenin', Mr Thorn.'

He turned to face Ed Stewart, a small time and mostly unsuccessful blagger. 'What are you hoping to nick today?'

'Don't be like that, Mr Thorn. I've got a sniff.'

'Use a handkerchief.'

'It's a good one.'

'If it's only as good as the last one, see a different chemist.' He stepped aside to avoid being hit by a trolley.

'Weren't my fault.' Stewart moved closer.

'You've been eating garlic by the hundredweight.'

'It's good for the health.'

'Yours, maybe, but not mine.'

'You want a handle for the Bracken Lane job?'

'Well?' Thorn feigned indifference, not wanting to encourage Stewart to expect too much from him in return, particularly when the last piece of information had been barely more than useless.

'It's worth a score.'

'What's the next laugh?' Thorn picked up`a box of truffles, walked over to the nearest cash desk, at which an elderly couple were unloading their trolley.

Stewart intercepted him as he reached the outside door after buying the chocolates. 'A fin, then, Mr Thorn.'

'You think I've won the lottery?'

'It's strong.'

'So's the garlic.' He brought a five-pound note out of a pocket, gave the other time to note the colours, concealed it in the palm of his hand. He left the building, walked across the large car park to his Ford. Stewart followed him.

'Gabby,' Stewart said, as Thorn pressed the key fob to unlock his car door.

'He doesn't have a longer name?'

There was no answer. Thorn handed over the note.

'Gabby Ayling.'

Thorn returned to the CID general room, entered in the informer's book the date, time, how much he'd paid Stewart and the information he'd been given. He went along to the detective sergeant's room. 'I've been given a possible name for the twirler in the Ansell job. Cost a bit, but likely it's worth that, despite his bad information last time.'

'Have you entered the details?' Frick wanted to be certain the rules had been observed before he learned the nature and possible value of the information.

'Gabby Ayling, an electronics wizard from Scotland.'

* * *

Ansell was watching a film on television, the ending of which was, for once, not readily discernible, when the phone rang. He went into the hall.

'It's Mary. We're just back and have heard the dreadful news about Eileen. We do wish there were some way in which we could help at so bitterly sad a time for you. She was so alive . . .'

Her commiserations continued. He gave conventional responses for a while, then let his mind drift amongst memories until she said, 'So I want you to come along.'

Something she said jerked his mind back to the present and made him aware he had not heard Mary's well-meant, but dull chatter. 'I'm sorry but I couldn't quite catch that.'

'You were struggling to understand why it had to happen. Can there ever be an answer? I was telling you I wanted you to come along to a small party. You're going to try to say "no", but you must not cut yourself off from the world. You need to meet people, to let them help you take yourself out of yourself. Sadness feeds on itself.'

Had she recently been reading a women's magazine? 'I'm afraid I'll be very poor company.' Ansell tried feebly to get out of the invitation. He couldn't think of anything worse than having to listen to her condolences and inane chatter – and to that of her no doubt similarly awful friends – for a whole party.

'People will understand. Come as you are. There'll be a small buffet. I promise you'll meet some charming people.'

He did not accept that some of her friends were 'charming'; they admired wealth, despised mere money.

He thanked her for the invitation, said he would try to turn up. On his return to the sitting room, the film had finished, irritatingly leaving the ending to his imagination.

Ansell was woken early the next morning by the repeated ringing of the front door bell, backed up by heavy pounding on the door. He went into the corridor and along to the road-side window, opened that, shouted out, 'What the hell are you up to?'

He then looked down onto the front garden below him. A police constable was standing there with Frick and Glover.

'Please let us in, Mr Ansell,' Glover called out.

'Why?'

'We have a search warrant for this property. If you will do as I ask, it will save us all a lot of trouble.'

Their calm politeness made his anger sound absurd. He put on a dressing gown – silk, highly patterned, bought in Hong Kong for Eileen, dismissed by her as tasteless – went downstairs. He switched off the alarm system, unlocked, unbolted and opened the front door.

Glover entered, followed by Frick and the constable. 'As I said, Mr Ansell, we have a search warrant for this house.' He held it out. 'Do you wish to read it?'

'To tear it up.'

'Unavailing and unwise.'

'What are you searching for?'

'Seven uncut diamonds.'

He wondered why they couldn't understand that had they ever been in his possession, he would have used them to save Melanie's life.

'We'll start upstairs.'

He watched them climb the stairs, enter the end bedroom. Standing in the hall, he heard the sounds of drawers being opened and closed, furniture being moved and returned to its original position.

Glover appeared on the landing. 'One room appears to be used as an office and has a free-standing safe in it. I should like you to come up and open it for us.'

'And if I tell you to go to hell?'

'I would say you are too intelligent to need me to answer.'

He went upstairs and into the study/bedroom they were all standing in, dialled in the number to open the safe. 'The only diamonds I have in here are very small and in the ring my wife was given when young, which she very seldom wore.'

'You will allow us to make certain of that.'

'Do you dig at the foot of rainbows?'

'Only white ones.'

The search continued for the next couple of hours until Glover acknowledged it was completed.

'Sorry to have disappointed you,' Ansell said sarcastically as he opened the front door to let the detectives out.

'I don't expect to meet success at the beginning of a case,' Glover replied, his meaning clear to the angry Ansell.

SIXTEEN

Frithton was still referred to as a market town, which suggested to those who did not know its present form that it was not very large. It had in the recent past been populated with a number of small shops run by their owners and selling goods and food of a quality now seldom seen in large stores, a weekly market at which cattle, sheep, chickens, rabbits dead and alive, game in season, and home-grown vegetables were auctioned, the Mothers' Union which ran a stall selling home-made jams and perhaps there would be a smaller stall run by a Bible society. In the past years, the town had almost doubled in size and most independent stores had vanished, as had the market.

DC Pascall parked behind a car which would soon have to be scrapped. Two young men, slouching their way along the pavement, noted him at the wheel of his car and after a quick comment from one of them, began to walk more quickly. He recognized the taller one with hair grown long and tied into a bun. Carter had broken into a country house, stolen a collection of silver and later, at a boot sale, tried to sell the silver to a constable in civvies who had printed out the list of the silver. Some were not born to succeed.

Pascall left the car, crossed the pavement to the front door of a terraced house which was in need of repainting and guttering repair. He knocked. The door was opened by a woman whose features marked a life of dreariness, whose clothes showed a lack of interest in her appearance. She looked past him, said nothing.

'Is Gabby in?' he asked.

She shook her head. The tangle of black, greasy hair hardly stirred.

'Where will I find him?'

She shrugged her shoulders.

'Come on, get the ideas working. You don't want us calling

every half hour to find out if he's turned up, making the neighbours wonder who he's blagged this time.'

'Them?' With the one word, she expressed her opinion of the neighbours.

'Don't make it difficult for the two of you.'

'You lot don't know nothing. He dropped three days ago.'

'He died?'

She slammed the door shut.

He returned to the car, cursed the lack of information which had caused him by his manner to appear to show contempt for her loss.

Back at the station, he reported to Frick. 'Saw his old woman and she says he died.'

Frick stared through the window at the summer weather – dull, grey cloud. 'It's beginning to smell like a dead-end case.'

Ansell phoned Mary three times to say he was sorry, he could not face a party; each time, the line was engaged. In a mood of self-pity and self-sacrifice, he went.

Maltone Lodge was on the edge of Frithton and beyond the garden were green fields and distant woodland. Mary sometimes decried the size of both house and garden to assure her listener that she was an ardent 'green' and would have preferred to live in a smaller property which would need much less energy. Neither she nor her husband would actually have contemplated leaving.

To another female, it was obvious that her dress had cost a small fortune, to those who recognized good jewellery, her diamond necklace, more of a fortune. To lessen the burden of having to arrange a 'small' party, she had engaged the services of caterers who provided food, drink, cutlery, crockery, glasses and staff. Had the ground not been so sodden, there would have been a marquee on the lawn and guests would have eaten and drunk while enjoying the soft sounds of falling water from the highly formal fountain imported from the seventeenth-century chateau in the Loire Valley. As it was, the centre of the party was the large hall, notable for the painting by Rubens (or so the nameplate claimed) and at the far end two knights in full armour.

'There you are!' Mary said, as Ansell entered.

'I am.' He tried to smile, not wanting to appear too discourteous.

'I was beginning to think you weren't coming.'

'You expect me to believe you've missed my absence?'

'Still the same, despite what's . . . I feel so sorry for you, David.'

'Thanks.' He knew he needed to accept her sympathy with more warmth and politeness; she meant well after all.

'You'll know most of the people here, or at least some of them, but I decided you had to meet someone who'd bring you some cheer, some light into your life. So come and meet her.'

'I'd rather . . .'

'She's the daughter of old friends of ours. A little bit feisty, but very much alive. There she is, in the red dress with her back to us. She's with those boring people, the Fentons, who can only talk about themselves. She'll be very glad to be moved on – it's surprising she hasn't done so of her own accord. Follow me.'

They eased their way between the many guests until she came to a stop by the Fentons. 'Sorry, Janet, but I must break you up. Belinda, I want you to meet my dear old friend, David.'

Belinda turned. Her surprise was as obvious as Ansell's.

'You know each other?' Mary asked, disappointed that it seemed the introduction was unnecessary.

'In a way,' Ansell answered.

'Neither of you has anything to drink.' She beckoned to a waiter. 'Tell him what you'd like. I must go and have a word with Julie.' She hurried away.

Ansell broke the silence. 'Time for the cliché apt for this sort of situation, more than just like "It's a small world".'

Belinda said nothing.

The waiter asked them what they would like to drink. They both chose champagne.

Conversation, after the waiter hurried away, was hesitant and sparse.

'Have you known Mary and Bart a long time?' Ansell asked.

'My parents are old friends of theirs.'

'Your parents are here?'

'On holiday.'

'Somewhere in Europe?'

'America.'

'Are they enjoying it?'

'Yes.'

The waiter returned, handed each of them a well-filled flute.

Ansell raised his glass. 'Am I allowed to drink to your health?'

'I'm sorry, but I'm finding the situation beyond my horizon.' Belinda admitted with a wry smile.

He drank, tried to find something more to say which would salvage their chance meeting. 'Have you been in the police long?'

'A few years.'

'Do you enjoy the work?'

'Most of the time.'

He drained his glass. A waiter, with a bottle of Dom Pérignon wrapped in a serviette, noted this and, having checked that Belinda had drunk very little, refilled Ansell's glass, and then moved on.

'It's not been all that long since women have been entitled to equal pay and rank in the police force, is it?' he said.

'Depends what you call "long". Look, do you mind if I go and have a word with Jill?' She did not wait for an answer and left.

He watched her until she was hidden by other guests. Mary had referred to her as feisty. He would have called her socially abrupt.

Persuaded to come to the party because the company would lighten his life, ironically introduced to someone who was potentially trying to destroy it.

He learned he had underestimated Mary's persistence. When guests were called to dinner in the large dining room whose mahogany D-end table on fourteen legs could have dined a regiment, he was seated next to Belinda.

They could ignore each other or find neutral ground. '"There is no armour against fate",' he said lightly. 'I read that when young and have remembered it ever since. Can't remember where it came from. Perhaps at the battle of Crecy and they were a French knight's last words, complaining against the English who did not know how to fight like gentlemen, knight on knight, not bowman against knight?'

Belinda merely gave Ansell a quizzical look and then turned back to the person on her other side with whom she was having a rather stilted conversation, it seemed.

The first dish was served. Scottish smoked salmon on one plate, two small wedges of lemon and thin buttered slices of brown bread on the second.

'Can I pass you the pepper?' he asked.

'No, thank you.' She barely turned her head to him in replying.

Her tone had been dismissive. He squeezed juice on to his three slices of salmon. 'I didn't choose to sit near you. You have to blame Mary who doesn't realize what you and your colleagues are trying to do to me, who won't believe I was in Oxford when—'

She interrupted him and spoke sharply. 'This is hardly the time or place to discuss the matter.' She turned back to her neighbour.

He ate another mouthful, spoke to the woman on his left. He endured lengthy descriptions of what her young daughter had recently said and done.

Belinda entered Frick's room first thing the next morning.

'Yes?' he muttered. The previous evening, he'd met up with a fellow DS, now with another division, and they had reminisced with the aid of half pints of real ale. Catherine, with whom he had lived since the death of his wife, had on his return offered little sympathy when he had complained how he was suffering.

'I thought you should know, sarge, I went to a party yesterday evening—'

'I have as little interest in what you did last night as in what you hope to do tonight.'

'I met Ansell.' She persevered.

'You keep poor company.'

'Mary, the hostess, knows him and thought it would cheer

him up if she introduced us and seated us next to each other at the meal.'

'I have enough work for half a dozen, a team who seem to think they're on holiday, and you want to tell me all about your social life?'

'I thought I ought to report the fact since he started trying to tell me he did not drive from Oxford on the Saturday.'

'He's getting rattled.'

'Drank too much champagne to remember his manners.'

'Didn't realize the circles you move in. What else did he say? That he couldn't remember Melanie?'

'I shut him up before he could carry on. Told him it wasn't the time or place to discuss the matter.'

'That must have got right up his nose and it gets right up mine. You chose to close him down when he wanted to lean on your shoulders and talk?'

'It was a party, sarge.'

'So?'

'One doesn't discuss anything like that at a party.'

'Pardon my social ignorance. I suppose it wouldn't have occurred to you that there was a chance he'd say something that could help open the case?'

'I've made a mistake—' Belinda started before being interrupted again.

'You manage to understand that?'

'A mistake in thinking I should report the matter to you.' She left.

He opened the top drawer of his desk, brought out a plastic bottle of soluble aspirin tablets and swallowed two. If only he'd stopped after the third or fourth half pint . . . The internal phone buzzed. Glover wanted to see him.

When he entered the other's room, Glover had the phone receiver to his ear and was listening far more than he was talking. Only after several minutes, did he replace the receiver. 'The CI at HQ having a moan.'

'Because the Ansell case isn't moving quickly enough?'

'What else?'

'I can't see why he doesn't understand nothing about it is straightforward.'

'Ring and tell him.'

Frick was annoyed. He'd only tried to offer a little sympathy.

'Why haven't I got your report on the Cahill case?'

'I put it on your desk earlier this morning, sir.'

'If you had done so, it would be there now.'

Frick belatedly remembered now that after arriving at the station and his office that morning he had needed a brief visit to the men's room. It had been his intention to put the report on the other's desk, but renewed disturbance in his brain and stomach had persuaded him to consider himself, not the work. And then he had got distracted. His brain just wasn't functioning quite as it should.

'Sorry Guv. I was on my way here with it, but was interrupted and somehow forgot to bring it along.'

'Provided your memory does not deteriorate much further perhaps you can remember to go and get it now.'

Sarcastic bastard, Frick thought as he left. Back in his room, he wondered whether to take another aspirin, decided that might constitute an overdose. No hypochondriac, he did look after his health. A glass of water should help replenish the dehydration though. After a quick slug of water, he picked up the report, returned to the DI's room.

'As far as you know and can remember, is everything calm for the moment?' Glover asked as he took the report.

'Except for someone who's acting stupid.'

Glover put the report down on his desk. 'Who's doing what?'

'Constable Draper went to a party given by friends with money – champagne, sit-down meal, servants – and met Ansell there.'

'That makes her stupid?'

'She sat next to him at the meal. He started moaning something about not having driven down from Oxford that day and instead of encouraging him to keep talking, she shut him up by saying it wasn't the time or place to discuss the case. If she'd had an ounce of brain, she'd have encouraged him to go on swilling champagne. He could easily have let slip something that would have helped us, the amount of champagne he was probably knocking back.'

'*If* he was guilty of his wife's death.'

'You're beginning to have doubts?' Frick looked incredulous.

'Not necessarily, just trying to stand back and look at the facts again. He's an intelligent man. If he knew the diamonds were in the monkey, wouldn't he have removed them on arrival at home and not left them in the monkey, lying on the bed. Then of what use would they have been to him, a complete novice? As someone unknown in the diamond trade, he should have realized that to try to find out who would cut and polish the stones would have aroused immediate suspicion. How would he have had the nous to leave the security system switched off to indicate a careless wife? There are a lot of unanswered questions.'

'One can learn a lot of the tricks from the telly.'

'Yet not gain the skill and nerve to carry them out. However, Ansell has to remain our prime suspect for his wife's death.' He became silent and the minutes passed by.

Frick waited.

'Josh, do you remember the Arnold case?'

Frick was surprised – and worried – by being called by his Christian name, something which usually only happened when the other was in a good mood because work was progressing well. Was Glover about to ask of him something he would not welcome?

'Arnold had a hell of a row with a woman which ended in his beating her up. She was in hospital for weeks, he was in jail for years because of previous convictions. During his time inside, he was made to meet the victim, following the theory that to learn the pain one has caused will make one feel remorse and shy away from brutality in the future. Could be possible, but things don't always work out as the experts decide they should. The medical profession prescribed thalidomide to alleviate the distresses of pregnancy after all.'

Frick failed to understand the significance of what had been said. Despite the extra aspirin, drums were still beating in his head and there was a choppy sea in his stomach.

Glover went on to explain his thinking. 'If at the party, Ansell was chatting away to Belinda, trying to persuade her of his innocence, there is the chance he will welcome seeing her again, hoping to make a further attempt to persuade her he was not responsible for his wife's death and—'

The phone rang. Glover answered the call, listened more than he spoke, eventually replaced the receiver. 'That was the superintendent, adding his moan. He would like to hear that we are making progress in the Eileen Ansell case before the end of the year.'

'So would we!' Frick replied with more feeling than his head could bear and the banging increased.

'He has just read an article in the local rag suggesting that, being a county force, we are not up to handling a case of this magnitude. Failing to achieve the success which would confound such uninformed criticism, he'd have to consider whether steps needed to be taken to ensure efficiency improves in C division's CID.'

'We're as good or better than any other division.'

'We're only as good as the last case. We have to start on another tack. Does Draper believe Ansell is searching for someone who'll believe him?'

'She didn't say that.'

'It seems very possible. So tell her to contact Ansell and apologize for her attitude at the party; it was just because she automatically wanted to avoid shop talk. She can tell him she's sorry for what she said and doesn't want him to think she begins to believe he was in any way involved in the diamond smuggling or in his wife's death.'

'Do . . . do what, guv?' Frick's surprise was great.

'You couldn't understand what I said?'

'You're asking her to be a . . . a double agent?'

'Hardly apposite. If she learns something important which enables us to open the case wide, she'll have done her duty.'

'What if she gets him to provide evidence which is strong enough to bring him to trial. The defence would claim entrapment.'

'You may well be correct if he provides direct evidence which is used in court; you are incorrect if she provides information which enables us to find and bring incriminating evidence to court. Then, the accusation of entrapment could not be sustained.'

'I don't like the idea.'

'A moment ago, you were blaming her for not letting him talk, now you condemn the idea.'

'Then, it was of his own accord. What you're suggesting means we would have gone out of our way to persuade him to talk.'

'Even a lawyer might find that too fine a difference for the average jury to understand. Here is a chance of learning if Ansell did become mixed up in the smuggling game, and whether he did frighten his wife to death as he tried to force her to say where she burned the monkey.'

'Sir, I appreciate that, but—'

'You will tell Constable Draper to make further contact with Ansell.'

SEVENTEEN

Why? Belinda asked herself as she drove along Huntston Road. She turned into Bracken Lane – and slowed. She had believed she had the right to refuse an order which went against her instinctive and ethical standards, yet she had not done so. Frick had been uneasy when he had told her to make contact with Ansell. Uneasy, she judged, because he considered it an underhand – and potentially career damaging – way to carry out the investigation. So why, knowing he would probably back her refusal to do as ordered, had she not refused?

She braked to a halt. Number thirty-four was no longer guarded by a PC, police tape had been removed, banks of flowers put on the pavement by neighbours had wilted. Other people's tragedies had short lives.

She turned off the engine. Had Glover or Frick given any heed as to how embarrassing this might be for her? Glover probably would not since the DCS was demanding action and that would override any personal concerns. Frick would probably not because embarrassment was a natural female weakness and peculiar to only the weaker sex in his view and therefore not an issue for him to consider.

If it had been a weekday, Ansell might have been at work and she could report no contact. But in the circumstances, what was the likelihood he would be back at work now anyway? Waiting didn't make an unwelcome task any easier. She left the car, crossed the pavement, opened the wrought iron gate, walked up the paved area to the front door. Her mother had said, when she had been a child and had had to swallow medicine, think it tastes delicious and it will. It had always tasted foul.

Mrs Kelton opened the door, a suspicious look on her face.

'Is Mr Ansell . . .?' Belinda began.

'Not here. Ain't you ever going to stop worrying him? D'you

need to be told what it's like, you lot upsetting him when he's mourning?'

'I wouldn't be here if I hadn't been ordered to be.'

She had spoken with such certainty that Mrs Kelton relaxed. 'No more would I be if he didn't need someone.'

'You're very kind to come here on a Sunday.'

'What day it is don't make no difference for him.'

'He's lucky to have you to help him.'

'That he is,' Mrs Kelton answered, foregoing modesty. 'You say you must have a word with him?'

'Yes.'

'Then he won't be long gone. You'd better come on in and wait.'

'I won't bother him for a second longer than I have to,' Belinda assured the protective cleaner as she entered through the front door. 'And come to that, it'll maybe bother me as much as him.'

Mrs Kelton looked curiously at Belinda.

'I've come to admit I made a mistake.'

'Which ain't the easiest thing to do!' She showed Belinda into the sitting room. 'I'll be away shortly. I've prepared a cold meal for him, seeing as I can't stay to cook because I must see Sophie's all right. Her mum and dad are out for the day.'

They heard a car door slam shut.

'That'll be him. I'll tell him about his grub on my way out.' Mrs Kelton left the room.

Judge an employer by how an employee speaks about him, Belinda thought.

There was a murmur of voices. Ansell entered. 'You've nothing better to do so you're here to ask more questions.' The anger was evident both in his tone and on his face. Their disbelief of his innocence in Eileen's death, his sense of loss and of guilt at not being able to prevent Melanie's appalling murder, all angered and unnerved him. And now the police wouldn't leave him alone.

'No, I've no questions.'

'Why then?'

'To apologize.'

'For what?'

'Being pretentiously pompous.'

'I don't think we're on the same wavelength.' Ansell looked thoroughly confused and rather weary.

'When we were at Mary's party, I suggested you were very ill-mannered to try to discuss certain matters at a party.'

'You were right. And that I tried to do so was more than ill-mannered, it was inexcusable. The apology is due from me.'

'Can we call it quits?'

'With pleasure. Now, the questions?'

'None.'

'Are you here merely to make an unnecessary apology?'

'Yes.'

'Are you on duty?'

There was the briefest pause. 'No.'

'Then would you like a drink?'

'I would.'

'I can't think why we're still standing. Please sit. I can offer gin, whisky, rum, Cinzano, sweet or bitter, and lager.'

'A sweet Cinzano please.'

'Ice?'

'Just a little.'

'Shan't be a moment.' He left.

She sat on the settee and faced a gilded overmantel mirror. Her hair was not exactly neat, she suddenly noticed; she should not have left the car window half open. She smoothed it down with her fingers. The collar of her blouse was not lying well on the jacket lapel; she straightened it.

He returned, handed her a glass, raised his. 'Salud!'

'Sante.'

They both smiled.

He crossed to the easy chair next to hers, sat. 'At the party, you must have decided I was a real . . .' He stopped abruptly, before continuing, 'Just caught the word in time!'

'No cause for concern. There isn't a four-letter one I don't hear every day.'

'It would have been a seven-letter word,' he countered with another smile.

'You have me temporarily guessing.' She smiled back.

They chatted; at first to break any silence, then with interest.

After more easy chatting, she looked at her watch, surprised that she'd been there so long. 'I must move.'

'Why the hurry when you're not on duty?'

'I have to meet someone.'

'You're sure you haven't time for another one?'

'Quite sure, thanks all the same, Mr Ansell.'

'Would you like to try David? Please?'

They went into the hall, then out to her car in front of the garage. He opened the driver's door for her. She hoped she did not appear surprised. None of her colleagues would have considered such a courtesy – she wanted to be considered equal, she could bloody well open her own car door.

He watched her drive away. She was one of those who were trying to dredge up evidence to send him to jail for crimes he had not committed, yet he had behaved as if she were an invited guest.

On her return to divisional HQ, Belinda went down to the canteen. She wasn't hungry, but needed time to try to find answers before she reported back to the bosses. The civilian worker served her sausages, very little mash at her request, beans, and jelly without a dollop of whipped cream.

She carried the tray across to a table and sat, too troubled to have noted she had sat herself down opposite Frick.

'Thought you must have lost your way coming back,' he said.

'He was out and I had to wait for him to return.'

'How did you make out?'

She put a piece of sausage into her mouth.

'Well?' he asked impatiently.

She tapped her cheek.

'If you finish before midnight, report upstairs.' He left.

Twenty minutes later, she had just sat at her desk when Thorn entered. 'What's got the sarge bellyaching?'

'Probably because I annoyed him.'

'You insisted it was your leg and not the table's he was

stroking?' Thorn laughed out loud at his – as far as he was concerned – very funny joke.

'Do you ever think of anything but sex?'

'Only when I have to. What have you cocked up this time?'

'He doesn't know it yet, but I felt sorry for someone.'

'No good offering that as an excuse since it's an emotion unknown to sergeants.'

'I suppose I have to see him and get it over with.'

'Say "no" and you'll be able to wear white at your wedding without blushing.'

'If I'm not back inside ten minutes, come along and tell me I'm urgently wanted on the phone in here.'

She left, went into Frick's room.

'How much have you learned?' he asked before she had sat down.

'Nothing relevant.'

'Why not?'

'I didn't ask questions because he was so down in the dumps,' Belinda admitted.

Frick's voice rose. 'Now I've heard the lot! Down in the dumps? He was shit-scared because we're closing in on him and that was the time to wrench the truth out of him. But you . . . you had to feel sorry for him and let him off the hook. You know what the guv'nor's going to do? Transfer you to a social unit so you can console every teenage yob who's frightened because he's stabbed someone for not giving him enough respect.'

'You don't understand . . .'

'Too right, I don't. Get out and find something to do that you can't cock up.'

He followed her, turned into the DI's office. Glover looked up from the papers on his desk on which he had been working.

'Constable Draper has returned from meeting Ansell, sir.'

'Has she learned anything useful?'

'She didn't question him.'

Glover leaned back in his chair. 'Did she give a reason or leave us to guess?'

'As far as I can make out,' Frick continued, 'she thought he was too emotionally disturbed to be worried by more questioning. As I've always said, she's not for the job. After all, that's not so difficult to understand. One can't expect a woman to take an emotionally detached view—'

'There's no need to itemize. You've made your opinion of female officers well known.'

'A man would have questioned Ansell even if he looked like he was ready for suicide. Knowing he was in a state, she should have realized he was more likely to crack.'

'She may have thought there was more to be gained by long-term sympathy rather than immediate pressure.'

'She won't have thought that far.'

'We'll move on. I want a check on the finances of Ansell and the wife.'

'But . . .'

'They're questions the CPS may throw at us and we need to be ready to provide answers or look slack. Does either have hefty capital and/or a private income? Did she have a life assurance policy? Has he been spending heavily, possibly on tarts or the horses? Did she have a toy boy who needed encouraging with handfuls of tenners?'

'Hardly likely. From all accounts, she was cold enough to depress a bulling male.'

'All accounts can be all wrong.' Glover returned to the papers on his desk and Frick was summarily discharged.

Back in his office, Frick called for Belinda.

He watched her enter. His wife had met her once at a divisional dance and announced her to be attractive, lively and fun. That was unusual. His wife's judgement had generally been more reliable than his own. 'What are you doing now?'

'Nothing much.'

'Why not?'

'You told me to find something to do that wasn't important.'

'Are you trying to be smart?'

'Just obeying orders.'

'Like questioning Ansell?'

'I've tried to explain. I judged that because of his state, there was more point in showing understanding now since that might make him more responsive later.'

'Are you going to tell me that's your idea?'

'Who else's?'

'You're to find out what the Ansells' financial circumstances were and are.'

'Why?'

'You are incapable of accepting an order without querying it?'

'I'm just asking the reason so I can judge how best to carry it out.'

'You do that by questioning whatever bank, solicitor, and accountant he uses.'

'Today's Sunday.'

She had not before heard him swear quite so expansively.

EIGHTEEN

Belinda was awakened by a shout up the stairs from her mother. Once again, her alarm had failed to sound because she had not switched it on. She hurriedly washed and dressed. As she made her way downstairs, the smell of egg and bacon cooking became strong. 'Sorry, but I just haven't time to eat,' she said, as she stepped into the kitchen.

'Nonsense!'

'I won't get to the station on time.'

'Then you'll be late.' Mrs Draper's manner, the progenitor of her daughter's, was always direct and ready to deny the supposed authority of authority. 'A cooked breakfast is the basis of good health.'

'And of excess weight.'

'Eggs and bacon are no more fattening than a slice of bread and butter.'

'If only!'

'The coffee's been through the filter so will you pour a couple of cups while I dish up.'

'Where's himself? In bed?'

'And probably snoring.'

'You shouldn't get up before you have to, just to cook my breakfast.'

'The prophet of self-decision is telling me what to do?'

Belinda smiled, brought two mugs out of one cupboard, teaspoons from a second, sugar from a third and milk from the refrigerator. She filled the mugs, carried them over to the small table in the corner, sat. She buttered one of the slices of toast from the silver-plated rack.

'There was a phone call for you when you were out last evening. Sorry, I forgot to tell you when you returned.'

'Who was it?'

'Peter.'

'Why the hell can't he understand that as it's over he really shouldn't call me all the time.'

'He made me wonder if it could be worth finding out if you two could live together again.'

'We couldn't.'

'A pity.'

'When you never really liked him?'

'Just a little too much self-confidence. Marriage can soon take care of that.'

'For you, it's a case of better a cocky son-in-law than none?'

'Marriage has its advantages.'

'For the male. Sex has to be on tap however one feels, cooked meals on demand, never a single word of recrimination when there's mud all over the newly-cleaned floor.'

'I hope you're just trying to be awkward.' Mrs Draper passed across the plate on which were egg on a slice of bread, and bacon. She sat opposite Belinda. 'Living here with two ageing parents must be boring.'

'A haven of calm after the chaos of work.'

'Hasn't any young man appeared to offer a more varied existence?'

'No.'

'Spoken very emphatically. Are all men temporarily off the screen or is there someone in the background?'

'Can't you stop going on about my non-existent love life?' She regretted her words. 'Sorry, Mother. I'm sounding like a bitch.'

'Not a description I would use.'

'Of course not since you haven't moved with the times. And I'm out of kilter because of a case.'

'Are you allowed to identify what that is?'

'In part, probably, the poor woman who was brutally tortured, carved up, and dumped in woods last month.'

'It's horrific to realize there are people who will commit such crimes. Is anyone suspected or shouldn't I ask?'

'As yet, not for that crime. But the case may be connected with another one in which someone is very much suspected, but . . .'

'But?'

'I can't believe he could be guilty.'

'Why not?'

'Because of the person he is. I'd swear he'd never so much as strike a woman let alone kill his wife by threatening to strangle her.'

'Haven't you told me when I say a photo of someone in the papers shows he's crooked, that appearance and apparent character are no guide to what a person is really like?' Belinda's mother asked perhaps sensing there was more to it than Belinda was letting on here.

'Normally, they're not, but . . .'

'You reckon occasionally they can be. Eat up, dear, or everything will be cold.'

Belinda put a dusting of salt on the egg, speared the yolk with a fork and spread it, then ate.

'You've always said the inspector is level-headed, so does he listen to what you have to say?'

'When it agrees with what he thinks. The fact is, almost all the evidence stacks up against David and the motto of the CID is that only facts count, suppositions don't. Yet if he did threaten her to try to make her tell him what he was so desperate to know and it seemed about to become violent, I'll never trust my instincts again.'

Belinda looked up at the wall clock. 'Shit! . . . Sorry for that!'

'Apologies for what I suppose is not even called swearing these days?'

'I've only five minutes to get to the station and the car's been acting stupid and trying not to start.'

'You haven't had a word with the garage?'

'Typically they say there's nothing wrong since the engine's warmed by the time I get there and when they try, it starts at once . . . Too much work in hand to bother.'

She finished the meal in two large mouthfuls and rushed out through the doorway, flinging on her coat as she did so.

As the car drew away, Mrs Draper refilled her mug. She wondered if the use of the Christian name, David, held any significance.

* * *

Monday was sunny; global warming, melting icebergs, growing pineapples in Sussex returned to the newspapers. The manager of the third bank Belinda rang was tight-lipped even by normal bank standards and would not say if David Ansell was a client, but suggested she came along and had a chat.

Flavin was pleasant and prepared to be helpful, but as she had already discovered, he observed every rule and regulation with determination. 'I am sorry, Constable Draper, but I am not at liberty to give you the information for which you ask without the requisite authorization.'

'Surely you can at least say whether he has an account with you?' she enquired.

'I am afraid not.'

'Suggesting I came here does make it seem he does have one.' Belinda tried to prise the information out of the unforthcoming bank manager, allowing him to circumvent his own strict rules without actually giving anything away.

'I must leave you to make such judgement. Return with the necessary authorization and I will give you all the assistance I can.'

'Thank you.' For very little, she silently added as she stood up to leave.

There was a knock on the door. A man in his middle twenties, his unusually high forehead drawing attention, entered.

'What is it, Jackson?'

'Sorry to interrupt, Mr Flavin, but someone said there was a detective here.'

'Constable Draper,' Flavin said, as he indicated Belinda while wondering why there should be an interest in her presence. He mentally and pessimistically propounded a discovery of fraud, a significant and perhaps criminal error in one of the clerks' accounts, a failure of the number of used notes being returned for destruction to match the figure accompanying them . . . 'Why do you ask?'

'To know if she'd want the box.'

'What box?'

'I've been helping with the checking of the contents of the vaults and there's a strongbox in the name of Mr and Mrs

Ansell. After what's happened, we thought the police might want to know about it.'

Flavin looked at Belinda.

'Yes. I'd like to see it,' she said.

'Will you bring it up here, please,' Flavin said.

Moments later, a medium-sized strongbox was placed on the desk after a newspaper had been spread out in preparation.

She used a handkerchief to check it was locked. 'Does the bank hold the keys?'

'No,' Flavin replied sharply. Had it done, he would have conceived circumstances in which it might be thought he had unlocked the box in order to see what it contained.

'I'll need to take this so I'll organize transport.'

'You'll need authorization.'

'Of course. Do you mind looking after it until I arrange things?'

'I hope that will not take too long?'

'I'll get it arranged as quickly as possible,' she assured him. 'And will you make certain no one else touches it?'

After she had left, the clerk said, 'Is it staying on your desk, Mr Flavin?'

'Because of what she said, I suppose it has to.'

The clerk did not leave.

'It doesn't need two of us to keep an eye on it,' Flavin said. 'You can return to work.'

'But . . .'

'What is delaying you?'

'I just wondered . . . Shouldn't you sign for the removal from the vault?'

Flavin was very annoyed that, because of unusual events, he had been sufficiently confused to ignore required protocol and, even more unwelcome, had been observed to do so.

Abbotts was met at divisional HQ by Glover. They went up to the conference room which had a slightly raised level at one end, large oblong table in the centre, blackboard on one wall, noticeboard on another, and a single window through which could be seen the unedifying view of part of a suburban road. Vane, a SOCO, a photographer, the two constables who had brought the strongbox from the bank, and a locksmith were waiting, the civilians with growing impatience. Abbotts and Glover finally entered, quickly followed by Belinda.

Told to open the strongbox after it had been checked for prints, the locksmith did so with such apparent ease, it would have seemed to anyone without the necessary experience that the locks had been weak. He replaced the tools he had used in the large leather folder and went to raise the lid.

'Leave it,' Glover said sharply.

'Sorry, mate,' was the resentful response. 'Is there anything more to do?'

'No.'

'I'll be off, then.'

He left, unregarded by any of those present.

DC Vane spread out on the unoccupied part of the table a square of specially prepared material which would catch and hold any particle, however small, even dust, which fell onto it. Gloved, he opened the lid of the strongbox and brought out an object wrapped up in newspaper. He placed that to the side of the strongbox, then lifted out the other contents which consisted of jewellery, which made those watching wonder what it was worth if genuine, and four files.

'Find out what's in the newspaper,' Abbotts ordered.

Vane carefully unwrapped the pages of newspaper to expose a fluffy toy monkey made from material.

Belinda exclaimed, 'That must be Georgie!'

'Good God!' Glover muttered.

'It would seem this was not expected,' Abbotts remarked ironically. He spoke to the SOCO. 'What about prints?'

'I'll go over the newspaper sheets later, sir. As to the monkey, I'll have a try, but with that fur, there'll only be one or two very small areas able to record.'

'Do we open up the ape, sir?' Glover asked, his mind accepting it might not contain diamonds, but hoping to hell it did.

'You suggest wasting time having it X-rayed?' Abbotts replied sharply.

'No, sir.'

There was fresh stitching on the base of the ape. Vane cut through this, eased out the contents on to the square of material. There were small pellets of foam and a plastic bag. The bag was checked for prints; there were none. It was opened. Seven irregularly shaped, dull, greasy 'pebbles', with not a glitter from any of them, were inside.

Each diamond was put into an exhibits bag; on the tag of each bag was written the time, date, place of discovery and then was signed by Glover.

'It seems,' Glover said as he and Belinda went up the stairs to the offices, 'that Sergeant Frick made a very valid point.'

She was silent.

'Intuition is as valid as yesterday's ticket to the Cup Final.'

They topped the stairs, walked along the corridor. Glover stopped by his office. 'I wonder what the lads at CPS will go for – murder or manslaughter?'

'You're presuming Ansell deposited the ape in the strongbox?'

'I doubt I'm being fanciful to think that since it was his strongbox in which the ape was found, that is a valid presumption.' He opened the door and went in.

She stood in the open doorway. Once seated, he looked up. 'Well?'

'There were several slits in the body of the ape, probably caused by a knife.'

'You may accept I noticed them.'

'Why was it stabbed?'

'Checking the diamonds were there.'

'Or were they an expression of hatred?'

'You are in an imaginative frame of mind?'

'I don't think so.'

'Then what are you suggesting?'

'That maybe this to some extent mirrors what happened in the old days.'

'Such as?'

'If you hated someone, you modelled him in clay, drove a knife or needle into the image to ensure his death or serious illness.'

'A very imaginative frame of mind.'

'We Aussies don't keep our minds tied down to the ground.'

'I thought you told me only one of your parents was Australian.'

'That's right.'

'Then I suggest whilst in England you respond only to your English genes and learn to show at least some respect for your seniors.'

'I bow each time I say, Yes my Lord Inspector.'

She was surprised when he laughed.

Ansell replaced the phone. He went along to the kitchen and larder, poured himself a gin and tonic, less strong than he wished because he had forgotten to buy another bottle of gin the previous day. The pressure of events was making him forget many things.

He settled in an armchair – one which Eileen had intended to replace because she had decided it had become shabby. He drank.

Detective Inspector Glover would be grateful if he was at the divisional HQ tomorrow morning at ten. He had asked the reason for the request. There were one or two matters to discuss . . . Such as? The speaker had replied that it wasn't possible to say what these were over the phone.

He had said he would be at work.

It was suggested that perhaps he would explain to his employers why he might be late?

Tell them the police wanted to question him and they would immediately, being PR men, assume he was heading for jail.

'And if I refuse?' he had asked.

'You might find reason to consider that to have been unwise, Mr Ansell.'

He returned to the larder, but the bottle of gin remained empty. He filled a small glass with sweet Cinzano. Mixing drinks might prove more efficacious than a second gin in rolling back reality. Back in the sitting room, he stared at the blank screen of the television set. Life was a roller-coaster. Having to accept he would never be a good novelist. A good position with the PR company. Marriage in the name of love. A less than cheerful, loving wife. An exhilerating relationship at sea. Having to accept Eileen could have told him where Georgie was and saved Melanie's and her own death.

NINETEEN

Ansell gave his name to the duty constable at the front desk, was shown into an interview room – dull, poorly furnished, the only reading matter a framed list of interviewees' rights.

Glover, closely followed by Belinda, entered. Glover offered a toneless greeting. Belinda, a more welcoming one. They sat, Ansell on one side of the table, Glover and Belinda on the other.

'We asked if you'd come along, Mr Ansell, to help us answer one or two questions,' Glover said.

Was ironic politeness their trademark? Ansell wondered.

'You have said on one or two occasions that you did not know Melanie Caine when you were both on the cruise ship, MV *Helios*?'

'Yes.'

'Would you like to alter this evidence in view of the fact that you have previously as good as admitted you knew her.'

'I have never said I did.'

'Your previous evidence would be an admission to most. The steward in Bar Orpheus on the *Helios* has sworn on oath that you and Miss Caine were frequently together in the bar; that you, in his opinion, enjoyed a very amorous friendship with her.'

His denial was immediate and sharp because Belinda was there and he did not want her to have to accept he had been duped by sex. A futile wish in the face of the evidence. 'He is either half-seas over or bloody well lying.'

'He has identified each of you from photographs.'

'Then he is lying.'

'Can you suggest why he should lie, knowing this was a police investigation and one in which he had no immediate interest and therefore no motive to lie?'

'People can say something without rhyme or reason for

doing so. In his case, perhaps it was the thought of possibly gaining publicity.'

'Did Melanie Caine telephone you at your home after the cruise was over?'

'She was hardly likely to have done so since we'd never met.'

'Telephonic records prove she did phone your home and the call was answered.'

'The records have to be wrong.'

'I think you should accept that that is very unlikely. Whilst on the cruise and berthed in Gibraltar, did you buy a tourist attraction in the form of a Barbary ape?'

He did not answer.

'Mrs Morley has mentioned that you did.'

'When she was not on the cruise?'

'Did you buy it for Miss Caine?'

'How often do I have to say I did not know her?'

'Then the ape was for your wife?'

'For myself.'

'You collect mementoes from your journeys?'

'Yes.'

'Then you will have a large number of them since I understand your job demands considerable travel. Where do you keep all such mementoes?'

Growing concern and panic began to negate common sense. 'In my house.'

'That was searched and there was no such collection. Did you buy the ape for Melanie Caine?'

'I've already said why that's impossible.'

'Did she handle it?'

'For God's sake, do you want me to write in six-inch high letters that I did not know her?'

'Mrs Morley has told us that when she saw the ape on your bed, she picked it up. On it was a scent which she had reason to be certain was not used by your wife.'

'Babs is a tittle-tattle and expert trouble raiser. When she hasn't any dirt to pass on, she makes it up.'

'She noted some blonde hairs on the ape. Your wife's hair was of a different shade. Where do you think those hairs came from?'

'Either the woman who sold it or Barbara's imagination.'

'Not from the woman who entrapped you on the *Helios*?'

'What d'you mean, "entrapped"?'

'After identifying you as a potential victim, she used sex to dull your wits until you did as she asked without thought as to why she asked.'

'That's ridiculous,' he said hoarsely as Belinda's presence again increased his sense of humiliation.

'Following information received, we applied for and were granted authority to open the strongbox deposited in the bank in your late wife's name and yours.'

'You listen to a woman who enjoys slandering people, accuse me of being persuaded to smuggle by a woman I never met, search my house, break into my strongbox . . . You must believe you're in a police state.'

'Who has the keys to the strongbox?'

'They're kept in the bottom drawer of the desk in the spare bedroom.'

'What was in the strongbox?'

'Important papers, pieces of jewellery my wife preferred not to keep in the house.'

'That is all? Please consider your answer very carefully.'

'I can consider it for the next week and it won't change.'

'When we opened the box, we found in addition to the articles you have mentioned, a parcel wrapped up in the pages of a newspaper which was dated after the Helios docked and your return home. What was in the parcel?'

'A ton of cannabis.'

'You gain nothing by giving absurd answers.'

'The question was meaningless so I gave a meaningless answer.'

'Inside the pages was a Barbary ape. On a small tab at the back of the neck is the name of the retailer in Gibraltar.'

Ansell's thoughts, already contused, swirled and collided. 'Are you trying to say it was Georgie?'

'That is what I believe.'

'It can't be,' he said wildly. 'If I had known he was in the box, d'you think I wouldn't have taken it . . .'

'To save Melanie?'

He forced his thoughts to calm. 'You can't find out who murdered my wife, so you try to put the blame on me. You bought another ape, had it sent here, wrapped it up in the back copy of a national newspaper . . .'

'You overestimate our resources and the ingenuity we are allowed to employ. Inside the ape was a bag in which were seven stones. We have asked an expert to examine them and if they are diamonds, to identify their source. If he tells me they are uncut diamonds which came from Sierra Leone, we will be able to trace their route from their source to the port – almost certainly Beirut – where Melanie took delivery of them and which you smuggled ashore here in the UK, for her.'

Ansell was silent.

'Is there anything you wish to say?'

'I did not kill Eileen, I was in Oxford.'

'Your denial and assertion are noted. After I have handed you your copy of the recording of this interview, you are free to leave. But you will please return as soon as possible with your passport.'

'I'll try to flee? As ridiculous as all the other possibilities.'

Glover addressed the tape recorder, gave the time the interview ended, started the rewinding of the tapes.

Ansell was handed one of the two tapes in a stout envelope.

'As soon as you like with the passport,' Glover said curtly.

Ansell left.

'You're wondering why I didn't arrest him,' Glover said challengingly.

'Yes,' Belinda answered.

Glover put the master tape in an exhibitions bag, wrote the identifying details. 'We still need the experts' evidence that the stones from the ape are diamonds and came from Sierra Leone in order to make the case against him as near watertight as we can.'

'You do accept there's room for doubt, then?'

'I'll accept defence counsel will do their best to find room. Our job is to make certain they fail.'

'But . . .'

'What?'

'Nothing.'

'You want to remind me again that he isn't the kind of man to threaten his wife so fiercely she dies?'

'He'd have pleaded, not threatened to throttle her if she wouldn't tell him the truth.'

'He could have pleaded all night and she wouldn't have told him.'

'If she'd collapsed, he'd have called for medical help. Can we prove he was not in the hotel in Oxford at the time of his wife's death?'

'Proving a negative is always difficult, sometimes impossible.'

'A ticket was needed to pass into or out of the hotel's underground car park. Has anyone checked the control unit to see if a car or cars left at a time which would allow him to leave the hotel and drive to his house and kill her? Have the bank staff been questioned to discover whether it was he who deposited the ape? Did you notice his expression when you told him he'd been entrapped by the Caine woman? He was really suffering from self-contempt.'

'Having to accept he had been picked up by a woman who drugged his commonsense with sex in order to make him do what she wanted is hardly cause for self-satisfaction.'

'From the way she must have gone about things, wouldn't nine men out of ten have leapt into her bunk?'

'If married?'

'Twice as quickly.'

'You understand our job is to expose guilt, not conceal it?'

'Are you trying to suggest something?'

'That your interest in Ansell's guilt or innocence is not bounded by the required standards of investigation. I am going to suggest Sergeant Frick relieves you of any further part in this case.'

'You demand success, not truth?' She turned and took a pace towards the door.

'Draper.'

She turned back.

'Justice is our only target. If the stones are not diamonds, we will re-examine the case from the beginning.'

She left. Am I being one bloody fool? she asked herself. I name David a man of honour – yet he gets hooked by a tart. Why have I been touting his innocence? I instinctively and briefly liked him when we met as guests at the party, then things soured; a liking which returned when I was detailed to make contact with him again. There is no feasible rationale to explain why one should like a dishonourable man; one turned into a smuggler by his own passions; one considered to have frightened his wife to death . . . How can I risk allowing instinct and emotion to override the moral code.

She went into the CID room, sat at her desk. The computer had been left switched on and the screen was showing slowly revolving circles. Her thoughts equally began to circle and with only a very small part of her mind on what she was actually doing, she began to type.

Trent entered in a rush. 'Have you heard the latest? The chief constable's retiring and they think Abbotts may take over. Can't decide whether that's bad or disastrous news.'

'Don't bother, it'll only be canteen cod's wallop.'

He came to a halt by her desk, leaned forward to read what was on the screen. She hurriedly pressed the delete button, but didn't have the cursor in the correct place, so Trent was able to see some of what she'd been writing.

He read out loud: '"There sits a fool who once more sought, yet knowing love oft comes to naught . . ." Is this the start of a bodice-ripping novel?'

'A seventy-year-old spinster's lament.'

'Yours?'

'I read it in a magazine.'

'And you have sympathy for her?'

'From the way she writes, she may have had the misfortune of meeting you.'

'I've just again been blasted by the skipper. What's got him in another lousy mood?

'Probably because I told him he was wrong.'

'You still haven't learned a superior is never wrong, just misunderstood?'

'He's waiting for confirmation the diamonds came from Sierra Leone before he arrests Ansell for the manslaughter of his wife and leaves the CPS to decide whether to increase the charge from manslaughter to murder.'

'So why argue against that?'

'The character of the man.'

'Which one?'

'Ansell.'

'What's there to argue about him? Shagged himself silly with Miss sexy Melanie Caine all the way around the Mediterranean, wanted to keep her in his sights, but needed to know where his wife had supposedly burned the ape if he was to succeed. The wife wasn't going to help him feed his passion, so in his excitement he scared her stiff. It's as simple as B following A and C following B.'

'I'm surprised you've managed to get that far down the alphabet.'

'Your tongue would make a razor feel blunt.'

'As you told me when I explained I was going to keep my pants on and not whip them off for you.'

'It was a case of unjust suspicion.'

'Advice to a non-starter.'

'How about a second chance now I'm older and wiser?'

'You never had a first chance. Sod off and try to find some work simple enough for you to attempt to do.'

He left. If a woman didn't quickly play, she wasn't worth the effort. So why did he hopefully still pursue her? He dismissed as nonsense the glimmer of an answer.

That evening, Barbara rang. 'How are things, David?' she asked.

'I suppose I'm still living,' Ansell replied.

'Are you eating properly?'

'I try to remember to use a fork, not the knife, with peas.'

'You're beginning to sound like your old self.'

Why not? All that had happened to disturb him was the death of his wife and the as yet unspoken allegation he was responsible for that.

'Are you eating enough?'

'Yes.'

'I want you to come and have lunch with us tomorrow so that I can be certain you are.'

'Thanks, but no can do.'

'The Leonards will be here and you get on so well with them. It's not right for you to be on your own.'

'Most of the time, I'm not. The police are keeping me company.'

'How d'you mean?'

'They seem to think I know more about what happened than I should.'

'You don't mean . . . They can't think . . .?'

'A policeman thinks whatever he thinks he should.'

She was silent for a short while, then said, 'I suppose . . . I mean, I can understand that you'd rather not meet people when for you things have become even more difficult. You'd find it so difficult to . . . But the moment the police stop stupidly bothering you, you must come over here.'

She said goodbye. He replaced the receiver. How long before his friends and acquaintances learned from her that the police were certain he had murdered Eileen because of another woman?

TWENTY

A clear sky and a gentle wind from the south provided a pleasant December morning. Anne placed a bowl of porridge and a small tin of Golden Syrup on the table.

Glover looked up from the newspaper he had been reading. 'Aren't you having any?'

'Off my menu since I finally had to accept how many calories there are in a spoonful of porridge.'

'It's the syrup. Try salt instead.'

'If you'll do the same.'

He read.

She sat, buttered a slice of toast. 'By the way, did I remember to mention Shirley's going skiing early in the New Year?'

'Since when did she learn to ski?'

'She hasn't which is why she's going. There's a place in Austria which is known for its beginners' slopes and the skill of the instructors.'

'Male or female instructors and skill in what?'

'It's our Christmas present to her.'

'For how many Christmases?'

'Have another spoonful of syrup, it might sweeten you at the expense of a couple of extra pounds around the tum. The trip is not expensive because it's a package; the hotel won't be luxury and après-ski will be jeans and a can of coke.'

'Who else is going?'

'Pamela, Brenda and a few others.'

'Are the others, boyfriends?'

'If you're going to start stamping, I'll go on up and tidy the bedrooms.'

'So Eric is one.'

'Do you know what my father said when I told him I was going to marry you?'

'Over the years, you've mentioned several versions. Which one is this going to be?'

'You were too young, too early into your career, and too self-confident. He was totally wrong, as all fathers are.' The coffee machine hissed. She stood, crossed the kitchen, poured out two cups of coffee, added milk and sugar, carried the cups to the table, sat. 'Darling, when are you going to take a break from work?'

'When I can.'

'We were due to go on holiday in the autumn, but had to cancel because of something or other.'

'The Jameson job. As soon as the pressure eases, I'll apply for what's due and we'll go somewhere.'

'When's that likely to be? When all the criminals also go on holiday?'

The emailed report was finally received on Thursday. Glover read it, put it down, looked up at Frick standing in front of the desk.

'If we'd written it ourselves, we couldn't have put it more to the point. We'll question Ansell this afternoon. Tell him to be here at three.'

'You'll arrest him?'

'Unless he can convince me the diamonds got into his strongbox by magic.'

'What d'you think the CPS will decide on, guv?'

'I'm still not going to guess. They'll have to reach a decision after considering several tricky questions. Did Ansell intend to use whatever means were necessary to make her tell him where she said she'd burned the ape? Was he careless as to the effect his threats might reasonably be expected to cause or was his intention to frighten her into telling him? Had he sufficient knowledge to understand extreme fright can occasionally cause death? Did he understand the need to cover himself by leaving the alarm system switched off?'

Ansell, hearing their approaching footsteps, moved out of the small alcove and met Glover and Frick by the front desk.

'Thank you for coming along,' Glover said.

'Had I thought I had an option, I would have stayed at home.'

'If you will follow me.'

They went into one of the interview rooms. Ansell had learned the routine – sitting on opposite sides of the table, switching on the recording unit, the preliminary establishing of place, date, time, persons present.

'Before we continue,' Glover said, 'do you wish to have your solicitor present, as is your right.'

'Why should I need him?'

'You do not wish to be represented?'

'I have just said not.'

'It is desirable to have a definite expression of intention.'

'Then I repeat, I do not need a solicitor to represent me.'

'Very well, Mr Ansell. We have received further information regarding the matter in hand, but before I deal with that, I should like you to confirm certain facts. Were you a passenger on MV *Helios* when she made a Mediterranean cruise which began on the ninth of June?'

'Yes.'

'While on it, did you meet Melanie Caine?'

They watched him as he remained silent.

'I will ask again. Did you meet a fellow passenger whose name was Melanie Caine?'

He accepted he could no longer deny that. When last questioned, desperate to prove his innocence, confused, he had betrayed himself. This time as well he didn't have to concern himself with feeling humiliated in front of DC Belinda Draper. 'Yes,' he finally admitted, gaining a strange, brief pseudo-relief from the admission.

'A fact you have denied on several occasions?'

'Because to admit it could make it seem I had been involved in her barbaric murder.'

'Were you in any way involved in her death?'

'No.'

'Because of your close friendship with Melanie Caine, did she at the end of the cruise ask you to take ashore a facsimile Barbary ape?'

'Yes.'

'Did you not wonder why she did not take it herself?'

'She said she had no room in her luggage because of all the clothes and gifts she had bought during the cruise.'

'She could have carried it in her hands since the ape is not large.'

'She must have thought that would make her look rather absurd. And . . .'

'Yes?'

'If I had to return it to her, I would have every reason to see her again.'

'You suggest she might have thought you would otherwise not have done so? Did you disembark with her?'

'I couldn't find her before I went ashore.'

'Neither your luggage nor you was searched by custom officers?'

'No.'

'Melanie Caine was strip-searched. Did that not make you wonder why?'

'I did not know she had been.'

'She did not tell you at a later date?'

'I did not see her again.'

'You had not agreed to meet after you had both passed through customs and immigration?'

'She didn't want to.'

'Did that concern you?'

'It puzzled mc.'

'You weren't worried it was a brush-off?'

'Not when she said she'd phone to say when and where we could meet.'

'You did not think perhaps she did not wish to be seen with you?'

'No.'

'It did not make you wonder if there was something more than foam in the ape?'

'Of course it didn't.'

'You arrived home and inadvisably left the ape on your bed. Your wife and Mrs Morley saw it there and Mrs Morley noticed the scent and blonde hairs, suggested to your wife you had had an affair on the ship?'

Ansell did not answer.

'Did Melanie Caine later contact you?'

'Yes.'

'How?'

'She phoned.'

'Where were you?'

'At home.'

'You had given her your number? You weren't worried your wife might query who she was?'

'I gave her my mobile and home numbers and a cover story – what to say if my wife answered the call.'

'Why did she phone you?'

'To say I must return Georgie to her immediately.'

'What did you do?'

'Went upstairs.'

'Why?'

'To make certain my wife who'd previously gone up wasn't listening to the conversation.'

'On the extension phone?'

'No.'

'You've told us you'd arranged things to hide the real reason for the call.'

'She'd have known from my voice that something had happened.'

'Did Miss Caine indicate who was threatening her?'

'No.'

'When the call ended, what did you do?'

'Went up to the bedroom to make certain Georgie was there.'

'You expected your wife to have moved it?'

'No. It was because . . . I was very frightened by the call and told myself . . . It'll sound ridiculous . . .'

'What did you tell yourself?'

'That if I touched him, she'd be alright.'

'And then?'

'I asked Eileen where she had put Georgie.'

'What did she answer?'

'She said she'd burned him.'

'Did you ask her where?'

'Yes.'

'But she wouldn't answer?'

'No, but I was certain it had to be in the garden.'

'Why?'

'Obviously she couldn't have had a bonfire elsewhere without creating interest, perhaps alarm.'

'Did you search the garden to confirm what she had told you?'

'At night, with the rain? And the way she spoke? I was certain she had to be telling the truth.'

'But she was not.'

'There had been so much hatred in her voice.'

'If Melanie asked you to carry the ape through customs because there was something valuable in it and she might have her luggage searched, what would you have done?'

'She didn't say that.'

'You are unwilling to answer my question?'

'To answer a hypothetical one.'

'I suggest you have been lying throughout this interview.'

'I've told you the truth.'

'You have admitted you lied to us during a previous interview.'

'I explained why.'

'Few liars limit their lies. You are lying when you say your wife told you she had burned the ape.'

'I am not.'

'I believe that a loose word, perhaps even a hint, on Melanie's part, convinced you she was using the ape to carry something valuable and illegal. That is why, when she asked you to carry it ashore and through customs, you agreed. You passed through customs without your luggage being searched. Had it been, had the ape been found, you would have pleaded ignorance and named her. Later, you deposited Georgie in your bank, convinced you were providing yourself with a generous financial future.

'We gained permission to open your strongbox. Inside, wrapped up in sheets of a British national newspaper dated after your arrival in England, was a material Barbary ape, bought in Gibraltar. Do you still deny you put Georgie in your strongbox in the bank?'

'I haven't put anything in the box since returning from the cruise.'

'There were seven uncut, illegally mined diamonds in the

ape. An expert has determined these came from Sierra Leone. It can be proved Melanie Caine was in possession of them when she returned to the *Helios* after meeting a man in a café in Beirut, that she was not carrying them when she arrived back here. You have admitted she gave you the ape to take ashore, that you did not later hand it to her; that when she phoned to say she desperately needed it to save her life, you falsely told her it had been burned by your wife.'

'Eileen told me what she'd done,' Ansell shouted. 'In God's name, how can you believe I wouldn't have got Georgie to Melanie to save her, even if the devil had been in the way? Why won't you believe me?'

'It is not easy to believe someone who has been forced to admit he has previously lied over a considerable time. I am arresting you, David Hugh Ansell, on suspicion of having reason to have caused the death of your wife.'

On instructions, Ansell followed Glover down to the charge room.

Police bail was granted.

TWENTY-ONE

Frick called Belinda into his room. 'The guv'nor's arrested Ansell.'

'I've heard.'

'You are to understand you will have no further contact with him, either in a professional position or socially.'

'Since when has he the right to tell me what to do in my own time?'

'You wouldn't catch a lifebelt if you were swimming for your life in the middle of the North Sea. He's trying to prevent you cocking up your career.'

'Or afraid I could prove he's made a mistake?'

'I'm buggered if I understand you, always making your life difficult for yourself.'

'There's no need for me to do that, other people manage it perfectly well enough.'

'You've been given his orders, so make of them what you will. Right now, get to this address and find out what the woman's been up to for the husband to beat the hell out of her.' He held out a sheet of paper.

'Is it a law in your life that a husband always has reason to beat up his wife?'

She left, went into the CID room to collect her jacket which was hanging behind her desk.

Trent, who was working at his computer, looked up at her and said, 'You look like you've just lost your knickers and can't remember where.'

'You make nonsense of the theory that men only think of sex ten times a day.'

'Those statistics are for men over seventy. Why the sniping? Have you been hauled over the coals for something?'

'I've been told whom I'm not allowed to talk to.'

'Never speak to royalty until they speak to you unless they're about to fall down a manhole. Who's trying to educate you?'

'The guv'nor.'

'He's only looking after your morals.'

'Get stuffed.'

'Is the subject of the embargo Ansell? He needs sympathy, not silence, since having bumped off his wife, he's a widower.'

'You're slightly more bearable going on about sex than trying to be humorous. Where's Britling Road, south Frithton?'

'Why go there?'

'To advise a wife to buy a baseball bat and knock the hell out of her husband.'

She left the inharmonious home in Britling Road after a wasted interview with a now contrite husband and forgiving wife, crossed the pavement and climbed into her car. If her parents had not shown her what was a happy marriage, work might have convinced her they were as rare as penguins in the Antarctic. Her bitterness at the range of matrimonial discords caused her to engage the wrong gear and the engine stalled. Further annoyance – at her incompetence – caused her to restart the engine and drive away without consulting the mirrors and collision with a passing car was only just avoided. The remainder of the drive was without incident. In her rash state of mind, she didn't think twice about where she was now headed.

Ansell opened the front door of number thirty-four, regarded her first with surprise, then reserve. 'The same old questions to find out which answers differ from the forty-ninth time?'

'No.'

'Fresh ones, then?'

'No.'

'Then what brings you here?'

'Being told not to have any further contact with you.'

'And you refuse to be told what not to do as enthusiastically as what to do?'

'I suppose. I'm getting cold in the wind. Are you going to ask me in?'

He stepped aside so that she could enter. She unbuttoned her coat and he helped her out of it, hung it on an old-fashioned stand. 'If you'd like to go into the sitting room, I'll make coffee in the kitchen.'

'I'm not allowed in there?'

'Your presence would be appreciated.'

They went in. She watched him pour beans into an elaborate machine.

'I hope I get things right,' he said, 'but there are so many dials I usually turn the wrong one or the right one in the wrong direction.'

'For someone professing incompetence, you seem to have a natural ability to know what to do!'

He laughed. 'Reserve your comments until you taste what's in the cup . . . I'd ask you to sit, but there aren't any chairs in here.'

She'd noticed the lack of any dining area.

He walked across to one of the wall cupboards above the work surfaces. 'Would you like some chocolate digestives?'

'Please.'

He opened the first cupboard's doors, searched. 'I thought they were in here, but it must be in one of the others.'

A second cupboard was equally empty of biscuits.

'Would I be correct,' she said, 'to think you don't spend much time in here except to make coffee?'

'You promised no questions.'

He found the biscuits in a third cupboard, as the coffee machine hissed. He set out cups, saucers, sugar, plates with biscuits on one, looked for and quickly found a tray.

'Can't we drink and eat in here?' she asked.

'Standing up?'

'You never eat or drink in here?'

'Eileen doesn't . . .' He stopped.

She moved until she could put a hand on his arm. 'Sorry, David. Let's go and be comfortable.'

They sat, facing the blocked fireplace and television set to the side of it. Their conversation was unforced, light, and sometimes amusing until she suddenly said, 'David, I want to ask one question.'

'Now the true reason for your coming here?'

'I told you what that was.'

'Who said you weren't to have contact with me?'

'The inspector; Glover.'

'D'you know why?'

'Because of what the sergeant had said to him.'

'Which was what?'

'Best left unsaid.'

'Presumably that I'd threatened Eileen in an effort to save Melanie?'

She said nothing.

'I've a confession to make . . .'

'Better not!' she answered quickly, her heart beating.

He continued regardless, determined to get it off his chest. 'With you having listened to me being questioned, learning I'd been targeted by a prostitute because she had judged me so bloody weak I'd do what she wanted, I felt and feel small enough, I could walk under an ant. I daren't think what kind of man you must now reckon me to be.'

'I'll tell you. Someone who made a fool of himself, but that doesn't make him any different from a hell of a lot of others; someone betrayed by circumstances, not character. Your home life hadn't been happy, had it?'

'No.'

'Would you have responded to Melanie if it had been?'

'She would not have chosen me.'

'You're not answering the question.'

'I should like to think I would not have done, but . . .'

'You are honest enough to admit doubt.'

'When one meets someone who recalls one's juvenile, erotic fantasies . . .'

'Imagination becomes dangerous.'

'Deadly . . . Belinda, I asked Eileen what she had done with Georgie because I was desperate to get him to Melanie to save her. I didn't have to threaten Eileen to make her answer, she rejoiced in telling me she'd burned the ape. She was so exultant that I had to believe her, as desperate as I was not to. I never thought she could have been viciously lying and had put him in the bank. I didn't realize how much Eileen had begun to want to hurt me . . . Our marriage soon became unhappy after our wedding, but I thought we'd learned how to live together.'

'Wouldn't it be better to leave the subject?'

'I want you to understand how things were, that she regarded intimacy as an unnecessary necessity . . .'

'Intimate details are best kept intimate'

'I'm trying to explain why I was so easily hoodwinked by Melanie.'

'David, unfortunately I remain a police officer. Tell me in detail why your marriage was unhappy, that Melanie had offered what you so missed, it must become more likely that you did threaten your wife when you were so desperate to know where the ape was in order to save Melanie.'

'You are going to report what I have just been saying?'

'Having been forbidden to have any communication with you, that would be to admit I was in your house, drinking coffee, eating biscuits.'

'Then whether or not I've dropped myself into the shit depends on where your loyalties lie and you're not certain what is the answer?'

She stood. 'I must go.' She hurried into the hall and by the time he reached her there, she had opened the front door and stepped outside. He watched her walk to her car, parked in front of the garage, climb into it and drive away.

He returned inside, sat. Sometimes, innocence seemed to become a weakness.

The front-door bell rang. He swore. Babs, come to reproach him for turning down her invitation and, in her inimitable style, leaving him even more defeated than when she had arrived. There was a second, prolonged ring. He returned to the hall, opened the door.

'Is your twelve bore loaded?' Belinda asked.

Surprise delayed his reply. 'Not even unholstered.'

'Hand guns are holstered, shot guns are cased. Am I allowed in again?'

He stepped back to let her enter.

'I had to come back because . . . I feared you could believe I'd entrapped you and would rush to pass on to the sarge or the DI what you told me. You were right. My loyalties have become divided and made me all confused . . . But I would not have passed on what you said about your private life.'

'It was contemptible of me to believe you might.' He thought she was going to speak again, but she did not. 'I've just poured myself another drink. Will you have a refill?'

'The liquid pipe of peace?'

She went into the sitting room, he into the kitchen. When he joined her, she was seated, her short, red skirt across her knees. Her head was turned so that she was partially in profile and he noted her chin was slightly too pronounced for her other features, an indication of her stubbornness, her readiness to face what she considered to be wrong or unjust.

'David, will you trust me?' she said, as he handed her a glass.

'Do you need the assurance?'

'I want to hear it because it means much to me.'

'I trust you, full stop.'

She was hardly the perfect police officer, she thought bitterly, accepting that her loyalty to the force was not absolute. 'Did you put the ape in your strongbox in the bank?'

'No.'

'How could it have got there?'

'Eileen.'

'She told you she had burned it, knowing or guessing what that would mean to you. Did she have a very vindictive nature?'

He drank. 'Difficult to answer. She was quick to find fault, blame, criticize, but I never did or said anything to have caused her to hate me.'

'You underestimate how a wife can feel when she believes her husband has had an affair. She saw it as a rejection of herself.'

There was a silence.

'Did you ever closely examine the ape?'

'No.'

'There are several cuts in the fabric of the body. If one disbelieves you, the assumption is you used a knife to try to learn if there was something solid inside. If one believes you, since she did not know about the diamonds, there is only one explanation for the cuts.'

'You're saying she "attacked" Georgie?'

'A childish gesture but adults under deep emotional stress often display them.'

'I have denied I was in any way responsible for Eileen's death; I never once struck her, I never once threatened her. But, as it must have done, my affair with Melanie so emotionally hurt her, that I provoked her into falsely saying she'd burned Georgie. That makes me in part responsible for her death as well as Melanie's.'

'You may have started the sequence of events, your wife had completed it when she told you she had burned the ape.'

'If I'd never allowed myself to become tied up with Melanie . . .'

'Ifs never alter anything. What might eventually help you to accept the past is if the man or men who broke into this house that night are identified, tried and convicted. Victims can often accept their tragedy has been brought to an end when those who were guilty are convicted.'

'What chance of that is there when everyone but you thinks no one broke in, but that I tried to make it seem they had in order to cover myself?'

'They believe you guilty; I believe you innocent. There has to be someone out there to identify. Did your wife give any indication of someone who was threatening her?'

'No.'

'Previously had she ever said she had cause to worry?'

'No.'

'Was there anyone on the *Helios* apart from the bar steward who could have noticed you were unusually friendly with Melanie?'

'I can only think of the man who shared the cabin. He remarked on it more than once.'

'What was his name?'

'I only remember him as "Call me Bert". He couldn't have had anything to do with what's happened.'

Never judge by appearance, she almost said, then silently asked herself, What in the hell am I doing when I accept his innocence? 'What was your cabin number?'

'Two six six.'

'Did he see the ape?'

'He was in the cabin when I packed it before going ashore and returning home.'

'Have you any idea where he lives?'

'None whatsoever.'

'When you were in Oxford the night your wife died, did you phone her?'

'I told one of your lot I didn't and he regarded that as highly suspicious.'

'A misunderstanding. Did you drive to Oxford?'

'Yes..'

'And parked at the hotel?'

'Yes, underground.'

'Was there a security man on watch?'

'No. There's the kind of automatic barrier one sees in public car parks – it needs a ticket issued by the hotel.'

'Is there a chance you may have kept that?'

'No.'

'So there's no way of proving you were there at the pertinent time unless someone saw you around – perhaps at the bar.'

'What are the odds of anyone remembering me when I can't remember anyone?'

'Poor.'

'Is that the end of your "one" question?'

'Yes, so I'll be on my way.'

'Would a rough supper tempt you to stay awhile?'

'How rough?'

'Lamb chops and trimmings. But no guarantee how things will turn out.'

'With your lack of knowing what goes on in the kitchen, I think tough might be an alternative description to rough. I'll don the apron.'

TWENTY-TWO

Belinda dialled. The connection was made and she was told to press one for this, two for that, three for something else.

Eventually, the 'Four Seasons' ceased. 'Rex Cruising Company. Can I help you?'

'Constable Draper, county police. I want to speak to someone about the passenger list of the *Helios* when—'

She was interrupted. 'You need Reservations.'

The 'Four Seasons' recommenced. Would she have to wait until Spring returned?

'Sarah Jones, speaking. You want to make a reservation? Please state the company's reference number for the cruise you wish to sail on and what type of berth you require.'

Belinda explained she required information concerning a passenger who had sailed on the *Helios* in June.

'You should have dialled nine.'

She expected to be put through to the correct destination, wasn't. She pressed nine, spoke to a man.

'We do not provide such information without a reason which we consider valid.'

She identified herself. 'This is an important police matter.'

'Very well. Will you kindly repeat your request?'

She did so.

'If you will give me your phone number, I'll ring back as soon as I have the answer.'

At four in the afternoon, Belinda was given a name and an address: Albert Crowhurst, Fontuna, Church Road, East Endley.

She phoned divisional HQ in East Endley, spoke to Sergeant Pace.

'This kind of job can take time,' Pace said.

A standard complaint which was easily countered. 'As did

a recent request from your lot. The guv'nor would be grateful for your help as this is priority.'

'It always is when it's another force.'

She spoke sweetly and Sergeant Pace said in a more friendly tone they would do as asked.

She replaced the receiver. It was probably a forlorn hope that Crowhurst could offer any useful information, but it had given Ansell a boost to know someone was trying to support him when she had told him what she intended to do.

Ansell just managed to catch the seven o'clock train whereas he normally made the earlier one and gained a seat; he had left the office later than usual because he was finding work difficult, his mind constantly asking questions it could not answer. Initially, he had to stand next to a man who disconcertingly spoke to himself in a low murmur. Ansell stared through the window at the London suburbs, streets of look-alike, architecturally barren houses. However dull the lives of those who lived in them, they were to be envied; the husbands would not be suspected of killing their wives, of being indirectly responsible for the horrific murder of a woman. Would Belinda be able to help him prove his innocence? Only she could because only she believed him. Why did she? Because she had an inbuilt distrust of settled judgements, responded to an instinctive belief not readily explainable?

The train slowed, came to a halt and, seen through a line of trees and beyond a road, was a large billboard on which was a colourful advertisement for a cream which smoothed facial skin, banished wrinkles, held age at bay. He had composed that last claim. Did anyone really believe it, had belief in advertising survived the plethora of advertisements?

The train drew into its first stop and many passengers got out on to the refurbished platform. He found a window seat, facing the direction of travel. Just before they cleared the city, he saw a section of the circling outside wall of a prison. How long before he saw that wall from the inside?

The drive to Bracken Lane was short and when life had been more structured, he had often walked to and from the station, but walking quickened the mind which increased imagination. He arrived at number thirty-four. A house which had been empty all day and so gained shadows all of its very own. On his return from work, Eileen had usually found reason to complain about something, but her presence had kept those shadows at bay.

He poured himself a drink, switched on the television, watched but noted little. Was there the chance he could escape suspicion before that became guilt? It was a proud boast that British justice was as good as that in any other country, yet occasionally an innocent person was unjustly convicted because innocence could never be a guarantee.

His mind wandered. What kind of a man was this Peter bloke Belinda had told him about? Belinda had spoken about his attempts to control and regulate her life and the breakup of their relationship without noticeable emotion. Had that relationship become as stilled as his own marriage; had its break-up left her emotionally battered, unable to understand how or why she had entered into it, very wary of any future one or even rejecting the possibility? Had she also suffered from such a lack of human emotion and affection as to render her childlike and naïve in all further attempts at relationships and so prone to the likes of Melanie Caine? Perhaps they deserved each other; perhaps they needed each other?

Detective Constable Younger – the name still provided stupid comments at work – knocked on the door of the terraced house. A child began to shout, another, to scream. The door was opened by a woman whose appearance was that of dull exhaustion. 'Mrs Crowhurst?' he asked.

'If that's what you likes to call me.'

A blubbing child ran out of the room to her right and put her arms around her mother's legs. 'What's the matter, Celly?'

'He bit me.'

A boy, slightly older than the girl, appeared in the doorway of the room. 'No, I didn't,' he shouted.

He ran past them and up the stairs. 'She hit me.'

'Kids!' Mrs Crawford added a few adjectives. She spoke to Younger. 'What d'you want?'

He identified himself. 'I'd like a word with your husband.'

'You reckon he'll be here with the pubs open? What's he done this time to have you around?'

'Nothing that'll worry you.'

'If what he did worried me, I've of been in a loony bin long since.'

'I only want to ask him about someone he met on a cruise.'

'That bleeding nonsense? Won a packet on the horses and spent the lot on cruising. When he said what he was going to do, I asked him what about the kids and me, how about spending some of the money on us instead of himself.'

Something was thrown down from the landing and landed on the floor.

'It's Betty,' the girl screamed. She let go of her mother and rushed to pick up the doll. 'He's bust her.'

'Little sod,' Mrs Crowhurst muttered.

Younger tried to hasten his departure. 'Can you suggest where your husband is?'

'Pissing away the money that's left.'

'Where's that likely to be?'

'The Dirty Duck.'

'Where's that?'

'End of the road, turn right.'

As he left, something more was thrown down from upstairs and the girl started to wail, her mother to swear.

The correct name of the pub was The White Swan; its nickname, a more accurate description. Younger entered, crossed to the bar, ordered half a pint of bitter. 'Is Crowhurst here?' he asked as he paid.

The bartender seemed not to have heard.

'It's only for a quiet chat.'

After a moment's reflection, he said, 'Playing darts.'

'Which one is he?'

'Looks like he's just climbed out of a dustbin.'

It was a reasonable description. Like his wife/partner, Crowhurst took little care over his appearance or personal hygiene. He needed a double seventeen to bring the game to a successful conclusion for his partner and himself. He threw and his dart ended up just outside the double circle. His partner swore, his opponents jeered. He turned to face Younger, identified him as a copper through an instinctive ability gained from years of experience.

The game finished two throws later. Younger looked at Crowhurst and jerked his head to indicate the outside, drained his glass, left. He sat behind the wheel of his car, briefly activated the sidelights. Crowhurst reluctantly crossed to the car, more reluctantly settled on the front passenger seat.

'Hear you've been cruising,' Younger said.

'Who's the sodding bastard trying to say that?'

'Cruising on a ship in the Mediterranean.'

'Oh!'

'Must've cost a fortune.'

'Won a slice on a belter.'

'How many times have I heard that after a quick in-and-out to nick a load of silver?'

'Ask 'em where I laid me bet.'

'When you tell me where that is.'

Crowhurst named the local office of a country-wide betting agency.

'Your missus is moaning about the cruise. Says you never give her and the kids any joy.'

'They ain't never given me nowt but grief.'

'A cruise isn't your usual line of business, so what were you after?'

'Wasn't after anything.'

'Hoping there'd be plenty to nick from people rich enough to see the world?'

'It's like . . .'

'Having trouble thinking up a reason which I'll believe?'

'Like when I was a kid and we was lucky if there was some bread to eat and I saw a travel film.'

'You'd money to go to the flics, then?'

'There was an exit-only door what could be worked from outside. Saw one of them travel shorts about the Mediterranean. The places were so beautiful, I said when I grew up, I'd see 'em for real.'

'An ambition achieved on the *Helios*. Shared a cabin on it, didn't you?'

'How d'you know what I did?'

'The lads down south told me.'

'I ain't never worked there.'

'Someone sliced up a woman.'

Crowhurst panicked and shouted his innocence, causing a couple who had just left the pub to check their walk, briefly stare at the car, hurry on.

'No one's saying you did. My interest is the bloke with you in the cabin in the boat.'

'He did the slicing?'

'South thinks he can help 'em find out who did and you being in the cabin means you can tell me about him.'

'When he looked at me like I was a piece of shit? And all he'd any time for was that toolbox he'd met and who helped him shag himself dry.'

'Did you see the Barbary ape he bought in Gibraltar?'

'Not until he was packing it.'

'Did he say who he'd bought it for?'

'Didn't say nothing.'

'Did you see him go ashore at the end of the trip?'

'No and didn't see her neither until she came out of the building after I'd had a mouthful on me mobile with a bloody fool who said he'd meet me and forgot. As I told him—'

'Not interested. Get back to her.'

'Surprised to see her around still. You know, there was something about her . . . Didn't hot you straight up, but kept you looking, made you think she could teach you a thing or two.'

'What happened when you saw her ashore?'

'A bloody great car was waiting and the driver got out and took the luggage from her and then they was off.'

'Did you know the driver?'

'No.'

'Would you recognize him?'

'Can't say.'

'Was anyone else in the car?'

'Didn't see no one.'

'You better look through some mug shots.'

'What for?'

'To put a name to the driver of the car.'

'It ain't worth me trying 'cause he was a long way off.'

'A look through the photos will shorten the distance. I'll get you another of what you're drinking before we move.'

'The old woman's expecting me back.'

'Not before tomorrow, she hopes.'

Forty minutes later, Crowhurst reluctantly opened another volume of photographs of convicted criminals and began to study these. It was accepted that a person's concentration wandered when he or she had continually looked at similar photographs for a long time and soon Younger called a halt.

The following morning, Crowhurst identified the driver of the car.

'Noyes,' Younger said reflectively. 'Doesn't ring any bells, but maybe Records down south will be able to put flesh on him.'

TWENTY-THREE

An unseasonably warm and sunny morning induced in most people a sense of well-being, but not in Frick. Seated behind his desk, he looked up at Belinda. 'Do you understand English?'

'Depends who speaks it,' she answered.

'What d'you think it bloody well meant when you were told to have nothing more to do with Ansell?'

'That the guv'nor was reaching too far.'

'You knew Ansell had been charged and you were told all contact between the two of you must cease. Yet you got in touch with him again.'

'Did I?'

'Don't try to play stupid. You're blind to orders because you're soft on him.'

'Hardly a comment you should make.'

'I'll make any sodding comment I want to. I've just seen an email written by a Constable Younger from up north, to you, and copied in to me as your superior. Huh! You know what it says?'

'Not until I read it.'

'"Enquiries being carried out. Info to follow." D'you want to say you didn't send that request?'

'No.'

'Enquiries regarding what?'

'If Crowhurst could provide any relevant information about Ansell and Melanie Caine when they were on the ship.'

'Who's Crowhurst?'

'Ansell's cabin mate. He might have learned something.'

'How d'you know about him?'

'The Rex Cruising Company gave me his name.'

'Because of your "friendship" with Ansell, you won't believe the evidence which says that to save the Melanie woman, he so terrified his wife, he caused her death. The guv'nor will likely have you up before a disciplinary hearing for disobeying orders.'

'For trying to get the case moving.'

'You're trying to say you . . .' His words became confused because of his anger, caused by her disobedience and by the possibility that when the case came to court, the defence, because of her friendship with Ansell, would be able to nullify the worth of some of the prosecution's evidence. 'Get out.'

The phone rang as Glover was about to return home and allow himself the unusual pleasure of lunch with Anne. Temptation said to leave the call unanswered, duty caused him to lift the receiver.

'Appleby, C div, Doncaster. How are things with you?'

The question was conventional since they had never met.

Moments later, Appleby said, 'I've a report which may bring a necessary bit of warmth to your day if it's like Siberia, as up here. A man named Crowhurst has identified one of the two men who met Melanie Caine at the docks. Steven Noyes.'

Glover recognized the name. 'Nightclub bouncer who landed a deuce for beating up a youngster?'

'That's the lad.'

'How safe is the ID?'

'As good as you'll get from a mug shot.'

After a further, brief conversation, the call ended. Glover sat back in his chair. He worked out immediately how this new piece of information had suddenly appeared. Clearly DC Draper had been doing a bit of extra-curricular questioning. But, lucky for her, it had turned up trumps. Records, hopefully, would provide the last known address of Noyes; if that was no longer valid, it could lead to his current one. He phoned Anne. 'Sorry, love . . .'

'You aren't going to make lunch. I'll see if I can find something else to have and hold the intended meal for tonight.'

He used the internal phone to call Frick to his room. 'Can you place Steven Noyes?'

Frick thought briefly. 'Yes.'

'I want him here.'

'Another GBH?'

'For questioning about the Ansell case.'

'Where's the tip from?' Frick asked, although he knew exactly where and the fact that Belinda had obviously tuned into something relevant annoyed him.

'A fellow passenger on the *Helios* who bunked in the same cabin as Ansell. He saw Melanie leave the shed, met by Noyes, and driven off.'

'And this man finally turned up to tell us?'

'No. Just imaginative intelligence.'

'I don't . . . Sorry, guv, I'm being slow. How did you manage to get this ID on Melanie Caine's acquaintance? How do we know the info is to be taken seriously?'

'As I said before, imaginative intelligence. Draper wondered who had shared the cabin with Ansell and whether he might have learned something relevant. She phoned the shipping company, learned the man's name and address, asked them up north to question him.'

Frick muttered something.

'You're concerned?'

'I should have known what was going on. Draper should have worked through me.' He didn't want to admit that he already knew that Belinda had been on to this strand of the investigation and that he'd decided not to tell Glover about it, assuming nothing was going to come of it.

'Perhaps she was worried how you'd accept her suggestion.'

Noyes, his facial features partially moulded by much of his life having been spent in the company of violence, watched Frick start the tape recorder. 'Why've you dragged me here?' he demanded, to show there was no reason for him to be suspected of anything.

'Thought it would be nice to have a chat and learn what you're doing these days,' Glover answered.

Noyes failed to conceal his uneasiness. 'I don't work the clubs no longer.'

'So what keeps you busy?'

'The odd job.'

'Like in the docks?'

'They ain't no good, me not being in the union.'

'Then you just drift there from time to time?'

'Ain't been near 'em in months.'

'So you didn't recently collect a young woman from the cruise ship, *Helios*?'

'Not me.'

'The car was a sharp limousine that'll have cost tens of Ks. Whose was it?'

'What are you on about?'

'Picking up Melanie Caine from the *Helios*.'

'Who's that?'

'You want us to believe you're only dumb when you want to be? What happened after you'd picked her up?'

'Wasn't there.'

'It was your twin brother? You took Melanie's luggage from her and saw her into the car.'

'That's shit.'

'Good manners.'

'Who's been talking crap?'

'A man who watched you meet her and then drive her away.'

'He's ghosting you.'

'Identified you from a mug shot, first glance.'

'It ain't easy to suss like that.'

'Happens all the time.'

'A bloke I knows was picked up for a sharp job because of a mug shot. Wasn't him and he had to do a stretch before he could prove that. Got compensation for being wrongfully put away.'

'You won't be cleared even if you borrow a halo. A witness, as straight as a laser beam, has come up with you meeting Melanie and there won't be a mouthpiece can shake him.'

'It weren't me.'

Glover addressed the recording unit. 'Mr Noyes has indicated that he needs a toilet break.' He gave the time, switched off.

Noyes said uneasily, 'Didn't say nothing about a leak. What's going on?'

'Thought you might like to understand where you sit. You met Melanie after the *Helios* docked and drove her away. Next thing, she's carved up and murdered. Even a halfwitted jury will accept what the prosecution is going to say. You wanted fun, so you drove Melanie out of town to somewhere nice and quiet. She had taste so didn't fancy a roll with you and tried to fight you off. You used a knife to calm her down and, as happens, became over excited. You stripped her of clothes, dropped her in the woods thinking she wouldn't be found until she was just a heap of anonymous bones.

'Because of what you did, the judge will send you down for long enough to make certain the only way you come out of jail is in a coffin.'

They waited.

Noyes muttered something unintelligible.

'Give yourself a break. Tell us what happened after you drove away from the docks. We'll let the judge know you helped us and he'll maybe give you an old age outside.' Glover switched on the recording machine, detailed the time. 'Mr Noyes, have you considered the likely consequences of you meeting Melanie Caine at the docks on her return from a cruise on the *Helios*, driving her away, and then her being found murdered?'

Noyes decided he was in the shit and if he weren't bird-brained, he'd struggle to climb out. 'He just said I was to go to the docks and pick up a bird.'

'Did he name her?'

'Never said nothing.'

'Who was "he"?'

'Never got told.'

'A pity. What did Melanie call him?'

'Pie.'

'If you're trying to two-time us . . .'

'I swear to God that's straight. She didn't call him nothing else.'

'Pie?'

'Yes.'

'Where's he from?'

'How would I know? Speaks English good, but there's a touch of the sun in him.'

'Where did you drive Melanie to?'

'Can't say.' Noyes noticed Glover's expression. 'Straight, I didn't know the place good and he just kept telling me turn right, turn left.'

'You ended up where?'

'At a house.'

'What kind?'

'In a row.'

'Terraced house?'

'If that's what you call 'em.'

'You went inside with them?'

'Was told to stay in the car.'

'Did you?'

'Yes.'

'How long were they inside?'

'Thought he'd never come out.'

'How did he look when he did?'

'Like when he went in.'

'What did he say?'

'Didn't.'

'You asked what he'd been doing?'

'He ain't the kind of bloke to ask.'

'Were his clothes disturbed, was there blood on them?'

'Didn't notice none.'

'He'd just sliced a woman to death and hadn't any blood on him?'

'I'm telling you I didn't look.'

Glover took a gamble. 'You did another job with him six days later.'

'Not me.'

'Bracken Lane. Number thirty-four.'

'Don't know nothing about it.'

'Your dabs say you do.'

For the first time, Noyes spoke with some confidence. 'You ain't got no dabs because . . .' He stopped abruptly.

'Because you were wearing gloves?'

There was another and longer pause.

'Did you threaten Mrs Ansell to death or was it Pie?'

Silence.

'If it was you, you'll be charged with her murder. And her

murder being tied up with Melanie's, you're lying when you say you never did the second job.'

Noyes would never finger a co-worker; that was, unless it was in his interests to do so.

'It was him, not me.'

'Carry on and explain how you broke in.'

'There was them others.'

'Name them.'

'Ain't seen any of 'em before. The twirler, he was real class.'

'And the others?'

'Just muscle.'

'So you three were redundant. Keep talking.'

'He wanted to know where she'd burned the monkey. She was scared so silly she couldn't talk and he puts his hand on her throat and says he'll throttle her if she don't tell. She went out like he'd been squeezing real hard.'

'What then?'

'Said I was to drive him to the airport.'

'Which?'

'Heathrow.'

'Where did he book to?'

'How would I know?'

'You telling me you didn't stay with him to find out so as you could shop him if that'd do you any good?'

'Don't work that way.'

'You know any other? What was his name?'

'I said.'

'Try again.'

'Pie.'

'Still seems too unlikely.'

'I'm telling it straight.'

'I'd have to be wearing shorts to accept that. I am going to arrest you on a charge of breaking and entering in the company of others, as yet unknown. You do not have to say anything . . .' He spoke the words automatically, his thoughts elsewhere; for Noyes, there was no need to listen, he knew them.

They went down to the charge room where the formal arrest was made. Noyes' pockets were emptied, his shoe laces and belt removed, placed in a bag. He was taken to a cell.

Back in the front room, Glover looked at his watch. 'Is the canteen still active?'

Frick answered. 'Only tea and coffee from the machines.'

'Would there be a meal in a pub?'

'Can't rightly say.'

'The Golden Goose does a good plate of Italian. We'll try there.'

They walked the four hundred yards to the public house. The barman said the kitchen staff had stopped serving, but might be persuaded to provide something. Publicans liked to keep on good terms with the police.

'See if they'll play after you've poured me a whisky and . . .' He looked at Frick.

'A half of bitter would go down a treat.'

They carried their drinks over to a table and sat below a poor painting of a nineteenth century man-of-war. They drank. Frick was the first to speak. 'Seemed like until we had that ID we weren't going to make it.'

'"*Audaces fortuna juvat.*"'

'How's that?'

'Fortune favours the brave. The only Latin I ever managed to learn. I was told it meant success with the girls.'

'The Romans knew a thing or two.'

In the early evening the next day, members of the CID were called to the conference room. Glover addressed them. 'I'm not going to waste time repeating what you already know, but will confirm what you already think. Melanie Caine's and Mrs Ansell's cases are stuck fast in the mud. We have learned the details of the crimes, but not the name of the man who organized the importation of the diamonds, who murdered Melanie because she was unable to produce the diamonds she had been carrying.

'We can accept it was the same man who organized the break-in at Ansell's home and, in her husband's absence, threatened to strangle her if she did not tell him where she had burned the ape. She suffered a vagal inhibition and died.

'We have the name of a man who has committed two murders and no idea of who he is other than that he is supposed to be called a name like Pie, may be a foreigner who speaks reasonable English, is of a very vicious nature.

'Unsurprisingly, the national and local media are remarking on our lack of progress; the chief super wonders if we are on holiday. So I am asking if we have missed something essential to the solution of the two cases.

'When you leave, read all the reports again, very thoroughly, listen to the interviews again, use your imaginations, think horizontally and if you come across any fact, any detail which has been overlooked but may be significant, shout it loud. I am unlikely to find it any more unlikely than some of the reports I have received in the past.'

A few chuckles.

'That is all I have to say. Can anyone add anything?'

Belinda stood. 'Sir.'

'Yes?'

'I began to wonder why Melanie called the ape Georgie. Mrs Greene told me that Melanie gave her the impression of disliking men, as to be expected, knowing her trade. So one might expect her to have chosen a female name. She led a hard life . . .'

'Wouldn't have done much if it had been a soft one,' someone called out.

'She would have had to accept she had a limited number of years in which she would work as profitably as she had been, then she would have to take to the streets.'

'Five quid a flicker,' said the same person.

'I should like to hear what the constable has to say.' Glover's remark was more threat than comment. 'Yes, Belinda?'

The use of her Christian name encouraged her to think Glover was ready to consider what she said and not automatically scorn it. 'It's common for people to name cats and dogs after someone they know or knew because that reminds them of a happy relationship or time. When Melanie was chosen to carry the illicit diamonds into England, she would have been paid a solid sum; nice, but not nearly enough to guarantee to keep her off the streets. But she believed the diamonds could do that. So she called the ape Georgie.'

Glover, who'd remained standing, put his right hand in his

trouser pocket and jiggled some coins. 'Grant that's possible, but how does it take us any further?'

'Guv, do you remember "Taffy was a Welshman"?'

He didn't answer.

'There's another nursery rhyme, "Georgie Porgie pudding and pie". I got to wondering if she had named the ape Georgie because someone with a name the same or very similar to one of those four was running her in the diamond racket. I rang the Rex Cruising Company and asked them to provide a full passenger list for the *Helios*' last cruise.'

'And?'

'They refused to do so.'

'I'll make certain we receive it.'

Glover called Belinda to his office. 'The passenger list is there.' He pointed at his desk.

'Any luck, guv?'

'You came up with the idea, so you can tell me whether your imagination had a field day.'

She picked up the three sheets of paper, read quickly, then again more slowly. 'Piera! Pronounce the i, as in "piper" and you start Pie . . . A K Piera was travelling on a Sierra Leone passport.'

'I'll give you a fifty-fifty chance of being right. Get on to someone at the airport who can provide details of what flight and to what destination, Piera, a Sierra Leonian, has recently flown.'

'Should I explain to the skipper what's happening?'

'In the circumstances, I think it will be better if I tell him. Sergeant Frick may be . . . How should I put it? Peeved, if you start telling him what you're about to do.'

Lufti Rorhart, of the Sierra Leone Selection Trust (Diamond area) looked across the desk at Kewsi Piera. He brought a handkerchief out of the pocket of his khaki shorts and brushed the sweat from his forehead, face and neck. It seemed to be a fact of air-conditioning that when the temperature rose still further, it would fail. 'The police in England wish to speak to you.'

Piera offered no response.

'I understand they believe you may be able to help them regarding the death of a woman who was tortured and murdered; additionally, you may be able to answer why a married woman suddenly died from shock.' Rorhart was a large man, in good physical condition. He laughed frequently, which caused some wrongly to judge he treated his work less seriously than many. 'What's made them think so?'

'How could I know?' Piera answered. He had a scar on his right cheek which marked an argument with an illegal miner who had demanded a better return for the diamonds he was offering. 'It's balls.'

'You have no knowledge concerning either crime?'

'None. Or of any others they can think up.'

'You will not, then, object to flying to England to convince them they're up a greasy pole?'

'Ain't no need to waste the time.'

'When in England, did you meet a woman by the name of Melanie Caine?'

'No.'

'They say you sailed on the *Helios* around the Mediterranean.'

'What if I did?'

'She was on that ship.'

'So were hundreds of other people.'

'And amongst them, Moses Dumbuya, who was keeping a low profile while watching Melanie Caine who was believed to be collecting the latest batch of illicitly mined diamonds from a courier in Beirut. We spoke to the English authorities to warn them she would be in possession of the diamonds. Unfortunately, a search on her arrival failed to find them.'

'Ain't any of that to do with me.'

'Then to keep them quiet, fly to England and prove them wrong.'

'Why should I bother?'

'Can't really say, unless . . . Do you remember Taylor-Smith?'

'No.'

'That's strange. He was from Freetown. A male ancestor was an Irishman which explained his name. He worked for us and received information which might identify the man who organized most of the exportation of illegally mined diamonds. Before he could name names, he had his throat cut. He questioned you shortly before he was murdered.'

'Crap.'

'I have his report in which he states he did.' Rorhart tapped a file on his desk. 'Because there was only his recent questioning of you to tie you in with his murder, it was presumed your evidence had to be accepted. But since England has given us details of your connection with the illegal diamond trade at their end, it becomes necessary to carry out a fuller, more thorough investigation into the presumption you were responsible directly or indirectly for the murder of Taylor-Smith. If, of course, you are in England to prove your innocence of any criminal activity there, you will not be here to assist us in our renewed investigation. I believe the quality of imprisonment there is considered preferable to here. You will decide whether to go voluntarily to England or stay here and help us. To allow you time to choose your course of action before we have your decision, we will first go to your home and search it.'

Two objects of interest were found in the top drawer of a locally designed and made chest-of-drawers in Piera's large and well-built house, a sharp contrast to others in the area. But for Rorhart, they would have been dismissed as of no consequence; he had learned that some criminals seemed compelled to keep mementoes of their crimes.

The knife was sent to the forensic laboratory in Freetown. There, the handles were removed from the blade; on the inside of these were, as Rorhart had hoped, stains which marked blood which had seeped between handle and blade and darkened.

Long, difficult, at times frustrating tests showed the stains to be of human blood from two individuals. DNA proved some had come from Taylor-Smith. A profile of the DNA from the second person was mailed to England, along with photos and a detailed description of an ornate locket that had been the second article of interest found in the chest-of-drawers.

'It's winter already,' Glover said, as Frick entered the room.

A gross exaggeration, but the driving rain which

intermittently lashed the windows as the gusting wind redirected it, made the remark seem feasible.

'A statement from Sierra Leone, sir,' Frick said, as he placed several sheets of paper on the desk.

Glover read them. 'Do we have Melanie Caine's DNA?'

'From the autopsy report.'

'And?'

'A match.'

'The locket?'

'Twin of the insurer's description and the photo of a piece of Mrs Ansell's jewellery. Her husband has told us that it was a gift from her mother and she constantly wore it. Piera must have seen it on the dressing table and nicked it.'

'So we've finally landed the bastard.'

'Only if he's released out there before he dies of old age.'

'I'll rest with that . . . Josh . . .' He stopped.

Frick waited for an unwelcome comment or order.

'You'll agree we've broken the case thanks to Belinda?'

'She's helped.'

'She should be congratulated.'

'We'd have got there without all that Georgie Porgie stuff. But I suppose . . .'

'She'll welcome a word or two from you.'

Frick left. Glover lit a cigarette. He opened his office window and leant out as he inhaled deeply. He was entitled to a forbidden pleasure.

Six minutes later, he reluctantly stubbed out what was left of the cigarette. He walked out of the room to meet Belinda making for the general room. He stopped her. 'Have you anything in hand which can't be left until tomorrow?'

'I don't think so.'

'Then perhaps you'll see Mr Ansell and tell him we have received information which clears him completely of having had any part in his wife's death or that of Melanie Caine and I will immediately be in touch with the CPS to tell them his arrest is to be revoked. Since he will have been under considerable stress, I do not expect you back here until tomorrow.'

She stepped forward and kissed him on the cheek, hurried along the corridor.

To a certain extent, he thought, Frick was right. Policewomen were different.

As she stepped into the hall at number thirty-four, Belinda said, 'I'm here to give you a message from the inspector.'

'Report at the police station at o nine hundred hours?' he suggested bitterly.

'There's fresh evidence which proves you had no part in your wife's death or that of Melanie Caine's; that you are completely innocent.'

He spoke slowly. 'Now I know what it's like to be told it was a mistake and one is not fatally ill. We must celebrate . . .' He stopped abruptly; he was ignoring her aversion to being told what to do.

She came forward, joined her hands behind his neck. 'Aren't you going to tell me how we must celebrate?'